THE DECEIVER
LYING LOW

First Published in Great Britain 2023 by Mirador Publishing

First edition: 2023

Any reference to real names and places is purely fictional and are constructs of the author. Any offence the references produce is unintentional and in no way reflects the reality of any locations or people involved.

ISBN: 978-1-915953-44-5

Mirador Publishing
10 Greenbrook Terrace
Taunton
Somerset
TA1 1UT

The Deceiver
Lying Low

John Adamson

THE INFORMER
THE INSIDER

FOREWORD

The Deceiver is the latest (and possibly final) instalment in what I think of as John Adamson's "Hub Trilogy". I'm not sure that John himself would describe the books this way, but the characters who first set up a Christian Centre called The Hub in The Informant *(Mirador, 2020)*, seeing it become more established in The Insider *(Mirador, 2022)*, now move to the continent in The Deceiver with the possibility of starting something similar on European soil. Each of the books works as a stand-alone story, but the connections between them provide an added dimension. Like its predecessors, The Deceiver presents Pete, Dot, Jack, et al. with a series of mysterious events that need to be disentangled before they can move forward.

John enjoys keeping us guessing as to how his plots are going to be resolved, but his books are more than simple whodunnits. As a committed Christian, John likes to bring faith-related issues into his stories, underlining that people's spiritual journeys are rarely straightforward. This "Christian" dimension of his stories is invariably linked to France in some way – probably because, back in the mists of time (sorry John!), he studied French at university.

In the case of The Deceiver, this "French connection" relates to the possibility of planting a church in the vicinity of Perros-Guirec, the seaside resort on the north coast of Brittany, famous for its pink granite rocks and sandy beaches. I think John has probably chosen this location because it's close to where an evangelical church-planting organisation called France-Mission first started its work in 1956.

The organisation I serve as UK Director – France Mission (without a hyphen) – was established in 1974 to support the activities of the French church-planting organisation France-Mission (with a hyphen). In more recent years, the French group has changed its name to Perspectives, but planting churches in those areas with little or no evangelical witness (of which there are many in France) has remained core to its identity. As Judy, one of the characters who lives in France, says in The Deceiver:

"France and Spain are actually part of the largest mission field in the world. Europe desperately needs the gospel." Of course, there's no shortage of ecclesiastical heritage in France but, as Roger (Judy's husband) rightly observes: "Beautiful churches with historic architecture everywhere you go, but life, heart and vibrancy? Like the congregation, they're hard to find."

Working in this kind of environment is hard enough for French nationals, but for British Christians (like Roger and Judy) who respond to the call to serve in France, the challenges are even greater.

Judy points out just how important home support is in such cases: "Knowing there are hundreds of supporters cheering us on year in and year out with their prayers and their financial support is huge. [...] They make a bigger difference than they will ever know."

And that's where France Mission comes in: we provide regular news and prayer updates for those with a heart for France and we also provide opportunities for English-speaking Christians from around the world to use the gift of generosity to help support the growing evangelical church in France. And, praise God, we're seeing some very encouraging results: the number of believers has increased from 50,000 to nearly 750,000 over the past 70 years and a new church is planted somewhere in France every 10 days. But there are still over 4,000 churches that need to be planted to reach the goal of "1 pour 10,000", that is, one evangelical church for every 10,000 people in France. And, over the next decade, the CNEF (National Council of French Evangelicals) estimates that an additional 1,000 pastors will need to be trained to keep up with the growth of demand in France.

These are huge challenges (miracle territory!), so, in France Mission, we seek to mobilise prayer, finances, and people to be part of the Lord's solution.

I'm very grateful to John for using his latest book to draw attention to some of these issues, but in a way that emerges naturally from the characters he's created – so much more engaging than a series of statistics! So, I do hope that you'll enjoy reading The Deceiver and, whether you have a passion for France or not, that you'll be encouraged to see the part we can all play in helping the Good News of Jesus become life-transforming for more and more people in our broken world.

Dr Paul Cooke
UK Director, France Mission

CHAPTER 1

Darkness was falling as a shadowy figure in a black hoodie emerged from the taxi and looked nervously both ways. She stared at the map on her phone before setting off towards her target location, shaking her head at the traffic as she decided not to cross.

"The Hub Christian Centre," she muttered. "That's where he is."

Nonchalance was not natural to the girl whose gait shouted self-consciousness and hesitancy. As she approached, still on the other side of the road, the door opened and two men came out.

"Maybe he's one of them." She upped her pace and hurried to the corner of the road before disappearing from the men's sight.

The older of the two men paused to lock the door whilst the other, a rather more rotund character, looked on. "An excellent evening, Pete. Very challenging."

Pete acted as MD of the Hub, although after recently stepping back from full time involvement, he now shared some of his load with his colleague and friend, Jack, an undertaker of many years' experience whose humour had cheered many a community event.

"Jack, in all confidence, I'm worried about Dot. She's under your scrutiny more than mine these days, so what's your view?"

"She's a good worker, Pete, there's no doubting her enthusiasm. She was a real find in my view, and still is. She and I have many a laugh together. What's bothering you?"

"It's not that, Jack. I agree with you. You manage her well. The thing is, she's not showing any signs of developing her faith."

"There's a good reason for that, Pete. She doesn't have one. We can't make her believe."

"Sorry, my friend, I put that rather clumsily. Of course we can't, I know that. She's stopped coming along to our meetings when we learn from scripture. She did attend at one time. Nowadays, she's too busy. Or at least she says she is."

"Managing the Hub has evolved, Pete. I have seen for myself how much more community work there is than in the early days. She's taken more and more on herself. She needs the money. She can't be burning the candle at both ends."

"I'm sure you are right, Jack. But there's more to it than that. It's been going on for a while now. She used to listen closely when I shared a gospel message with her on a one-to-one basis, but these days she sometimes turns quite angry. It's like she's changed. Or is it me? Am I getting things wrong now I'm around a bit less?"

"No, I've noticed it too. It began after Sid left the scene, almost as if she thought God had taken him away from her. But it doesn't hinder her daily work, from what I can see. It's not a problem if she directs her comments to you and me, surely?"

"Not as such, Jack. When Sid appeared in the Hub, she did appear to take an interest in the man."

"There was plenty of evidence for that at the time, Pete."

"That's right. But was his departure really the cause of such a change in attitude? Do you think it was, Jack?"

"Quite likely, yes. But it's not always a bad sign. Remember that when the gospel makes an impact on a person, it sometimes brings a rebellion before acceptance appears on the horizon."

"True, Jack, we've seen that before. But when we have new Christians here who are at the beginning of their own journey, it would be more than confusing if a member of our staff started creating doubts for them. As leaders, we have a responsibility to see that it doesn't happen. The aim of the Hub is to ultimately encourage people to faith."

"And that includes Dot. So what are you suggesting we do, Pete? She's going to be very hard to replace, never mind the ethics of sacking the poor woman. She's never had a day off sick and she worked all her holidays in recent times."

"Jack, years ago, my mother created this organisation to enable people to find Jesus. She was key to the whole project. I am here, part time or not, to honour her vision. Whatever else we may do, that is our fundamental purpose. So firstly, we need to continue to pray for Dot."

"Agreed. Secondly?"

"How do you get on with her, Jack?"

"Fine. We're honest with each other. She's become a friend."

"Do you still try to share the gospel with her?"

"Pete, of course I do, and you do know it's not that easy. Do it the wrong way or at the wrong time and it has the opposite effect."

"I know, Jack. I suspect I've been guilty of that with her. I forget that God reaches out to people in his own time, and it's me that tries to speed him up. But I may have done it once too often and have burned my boats with Dot."

"I am sensing a task heading my way!" Jack grinned.

"Well, we all love your funny stories, and you might be able to help her back to being on track. Who knows? And I'll back off, Jack."

"She needs a bloke, Pete. Like we said, it's a shame Sid's no longer around."

"True, although some in our wider community would ask if God would want her involved with an ex-con? They would also suggest that a more straightforward chap might be better."

"They'd be wrong. He's been saved, Pete. And he would have solved her money issues."

"Pray, Jack. Pray. God can have a funny way of working things out, using the most unexpected people."

Jack nodded. "Even the likes of me. I'll tell her about tonight's session when I get a chance. That's relevant, being about a man who was despised. Money issues too. Might resonate with Dot. Listen, Pete, I'm a tired old Hector. See you soon. I'm off."

"Goodnight, my friend. I'll see you next week. As I told you, I'm taking a few days off."

As Jack walked to his car, there was a flash from a mobile phone camera which made him jump. He looked around but didn't see the hoodie or its wearer in a doorway across the road.

The next morning, Dot bustled into the Hub kitchen, and stared at the figure who was helping himself to the French bread. "What are you up to, Jack? You know the rules. Just because the big boss is taking time off this week, they still apply. Catering staff only. And it's for the warm spaces lunch, not hungry undertakers like you."

Jack grinned sheepishly. "I'm starving. I got called into work at breakfast time and couldn't face any food after embalming a murderer who only ate cornflakes."

Dot knew her friend well. "Not the cereal killer? Enough! Out!"

He straightened his face with a resigned look before exiting to the customer side of the hatch, then leaned over to regain her attention. "Dot, many many moons ago, a baguette was lying forlornly in a small and uninspiring zoo cage. What was written on the sign above the cage?"

"I'm going to regret saying this, but go on, tell me."

Jack smiled. "Three words, 'Bread in Captivity'."

She laughed and made to get on with her work.

Jack hadn't finished. "You missed a good worship session here last night, Dot."

"How long did the speaker go on for?" Dot cut to the chase.

"Not too long. Not like the old boy from down south that time a month or so ago who was over an hour."

"I think you told me. Wasn't he trying to recruit some scousers to help at an evangelistic summer English Language camp for Hong Kong kids in Kent?"

"Yes, that's the one. He didn't know half of the problems he would have ended up with. Great cause, wrong area of the country. Separated by a common tongue, and that's before the students arrive. He went on and on. Wouldn't give up the microphone."

"Didn't the tech guy switch him off eventually?"

"That's right. The music group sang 'The Day Thou Gavest Lord is Ended' with a passion they had previously never discovered, and then my favourite mission night song."

"Remind me, Jack."

"It's beautiful, Dot. It starts 'Take my Wife and Let me Be'. I might not have the words exactly right, though."

"So how did last night's oration go down?"

"Well, very well. The speaker told a cracking story about how things aren't always what they seem."

"Always? I'd say never. How was that linked to the Bible? I presume it was."

"Let me tell you the story first. It's about another couple of cages at the same nineteenth century zoo."

"Sounds fascinating." Dot feigned a yawn. "I'll be listening while I make you a quick sandwich."

Jack's fresh grin was warm. "So back then, a zoo was just about curious tourists coming to see animals they had only heard of. And this one brought them in by the thousand, so it - and its owner - prospered."

Dot turned her head towards him. "I'm guessing he had a star attraction. I've read a few things about those days."

"You're right. He had the most amazing gorilla. The trainer was a former gymnast. Let's call him Pete."

Dot sniggered. Pete was the son of the Christian woman

who had inspired them to bring hope in every sense through this urban community hub, and she respected his leadership. He was a good boss.

Jack went on. "So gorilla-trainer Pete aimed simply to take the animal's natural talents to the next level. He and the monkey were bezzies, and the beast responded like a champion. The gorilla's forward roll was followed by a fabulous forerunner of the Fosbury flop over a branch. The double reverse pike at the top of the tree was the climax of the act. The crowds roared their delight, and the owner's smile grew larger, along with his wallet. The good times rolled on for four years."

"He'd be the sort of chap I need to meet!" Dot's eyes lit up.

Jack continued. "Then late one night, a messenger arrived, summoning Pete to the boss's office. The words he dreaded greeted him, telling him that the gorilla was dead.

Pete gulped and asked his boss, between sobs, what they were going to do. The boss looked at him and explained that they could not possibly let down the thousands of customers expected at nine."

Dot put the butter knife down. "Tricky situation, Jack."

"It was, Dot. Even the gymnast-turned trainer was perplexed. He made that clear. He stared at his boss and told him that he couldn't teach a new one in a matter of hours."

Dot nodded and reached for more bread. "I hope the boss agreed!"

Jack indicated in the affirmative. "Yes, he gave Pete a gorilla costume and told him that he was to be the gorilla. Then he sent him to the cage to start practising."

Dot grinned. "He must have been nervous about what was to come."

"Nervous? He was totally shaken, but he donned the outfit and did as he was told. His gymnastic instincts returned. His confidence grew. Dot, Pete was going to go for it."

Dot glanced at Jack. "I thought he might."

Jack carried on. "Warming up was intense but positive. At nine, as the crowds looked on, Pete began the routine. They cheered. He pushed himself to his limits and they roared, so he went for it. The triple pike off the top branch, the move the gorilla never attempted. Alas, Pete's paw slipped at the crucial moment. He flew out of the cage, landing in a heap in the lion's enclosure."

"Oh no!" Dot stopped working. "Whatever happened next, Jack?"

"Well, the lion looked up, licked his lips and padded across towards Pete. The latter was shaking but made not a sound. The lion approached. At three metres away, Pete cracked. "Help!" The voice was tiny. The lion paused and took another step. "Help!" exclaimed Pete, more loudly. The big cat paused before pushing his face into Pete's. He cried out with all the volume he could muster. "HELP!" "Shut up you idiot!" said the lion, "You'll get both of us the sack!"".

Dot laughed. "I suppose you'll tell me what happened to the baguette now."

Jack affected reluctance. "The baguette? It went mouldy, but the owner had plenty of dough."

His friend grinned briefly. "I wouldn't have minded meeting him then. What was the speaker's point? You're bound to want to tell me."

"Our busy way of life leaves us taking too much for granted. We make assumptions which are fundamentally wrong, then base our lives on them. And sometimes we can be deliberately misled."

"And the Bible?"

"If we all lived according to God's law, truth would triumph and we would have real security in our choice of behaviour. Lies and deceit stem from human hearts and fickle man-made rules which are exploited by the devil."

"Ah. Like abortion laws?"

"Like everything. The planet, greed, the sense of over-entitlement which the rich have at the expense of the poor, the way we treat each other, materialism, euthanasia, abortion, what we see as our rights, everything."

"That speaker's going to upset a lot of people, I'll say that for him."

"Why do you assume it was a man, Dot? It was a woman, actually, one who'd been through the mill a few times. She described being overwhelmed by the immensity of God's love when she turned to him after all her struggles."

"And where's she in the Bible?"

"Everywhere. We're all in the Bible, whoever we are and wherever we live. You'll find yourself there one day, Dot."

"I meant her point about assumptions."

"That's in a few places. She used a story from Luke's gospel. She actually looked at how Jesus dealt with sinners. It was about Zacchaeus. He was a tax collector, a Jewish man who collaborated by enforcing tax legislation for the occupying Roman forces. He was hated by his own people for another issue too. He charged the Jews way more than he had to pay the Romans, so he lined his own pocket. The weaker they were, the more he exploited them. He operated a scam."

Dot passed the sandwich over to Jack. "Horrible man. But that's not about perceptions. I don't see your point."

"Hang on, Dot. Think about Zacchaeus the scammer. What were his perceptions of Jesus? An interfering troublemaker who was giving off signals that he thought he was God? Someone whom the Jewish leaders were disrespecting? A threat to the established order of which he, Zac, was a key part?"

"His livelihood was at stake, I guess."

"Don't you see, Dot? He realised he needed to take the claims of Jesus seriously. For him, that meant reassessing his perceptions. We all need to do that ourselves, re-evaluate our views and opinions and the way we operate, as Zacchaeus did."

Dot contorted her face to display incredulity. "I need to get on."

"Dot, see how Jesus reacted. He went to Zac's house and had dinner with him. The establishment figures railed in horror. People just didn't mix with those they called sinners, but Jesus did. His perceptions of people are very different to ours."

"I've got all the food to prepare for lunch, Jack. I'm busy. Every single day. I haven't had a holiday for four years now, I have a living to earn and you know how tough life has become since all the prices went up. I'm struggling to get by. I simply don't have time to work your riddles out."

"Sorry, Dot, I just want the best for you. I don't mean to go on. You must be fed up with me."

"No, Jack, I know all that. I had Pete on my case the other

day, talking about how God has changed a friend of his who suffered terrible abuse as a child."

"It was really awful. That'll be Roger's wife. Did he say she was called Judy?"

"It was her, for sure, Jack, and I remember her well. I met her at the airport for starters."

"Then she was there for the shooting. Sorry, Dot. I'd forgotten."

"No worries, Jack. Apparently, she's like a new person these days, full of confidence, according to Pete. I'm glad for her, mind, really I am, but I don't know I'd cope if she took it on herself to convert me too."

"They're in France. Probably unlikely to drop in at Warm Spaces here for coffee."

"Ok, Jack, I get it. And I'm sorry if I overreact at times. Pete says I do. I can't help it."

"No worries, Dot, you and I won't fall out over it. I'll leave you to press on. I won't disturb you further. Anyway I've asked Maria to meet me for a chat."

Dot's curiosity got the better of her urge to crack on. "Maria? Who's that?"

"My god-daughter."

Dot put a pile of plates down. "You've not mentioned her before. Aren't you a bit old for that kind of thing? How old is she anyway? It's a weekday. Shouldn't she be in school?"

Jack laughed. "She's twenty-three. And it's quite new. Her father claimed that he came to a few meetings here during that outreach week soon after you started here, but not with Maria."

Dot nodded. "Go on, Jack."

"It's all a bit unofficial to be honest. Her dad asked me to pray for her. She's been in a lot of trouble."

"I don't get why you haven't mentioned her though, Jack."

"It's all rather delicate, Dot. It was a few days after the event ended, a text message from a number I didn't know, said he was a bloke who'd been in my group, then just the prayer request and her name, so I replied and said I would be pleased to act like a godfather to her."

"And did he reply?"

"Barely. Except her first name and an email address. And a word in upper case. CONFIDENTIAL. I wrote her a message saying her father had asked me to pray for her, but no reply came, for more months than I care to remember."

"You didn't pray for her. Isn't that wrong? I thought you Christians prayed for everything. Not that much seems to happen when you do, in my view."

Jack ignored the jibe. "I did, Dot. Silently. And every day. I've got one idea as to who it might be, but no way of knowing for sure. There was no answer when I asked. It's rather mysterious."

"I can't help you there, I really can't recall the individuals who attended. No idea. It's another of your riddles. I take it this Maria has been in touch recently then?"

"A request for help. One sentence. I asked her to meet me here today around now."

Dot resumed her work, clattering the tableware to discourage further attention from her friend.

Jack's phone pinged and he muttered under his breath. "Ok, not today, Maria. Tomorrow." He left Dot and headed for the funeral parlour.

CHAPTER 2

It wasn't tomorrow, nor the day after. On the third day, Jack returned to find Dot in her element. The foodbank was in full swing, and a group chair exercise session for the more mature members of the community was coming to a close before Dot served the lunch. Jack took a seat by the window.

To his relief, he was not alone for long. A hard-faced young woman with blue hair opened the door and looked around before checking. "You Jack? I think you are." Her accent was from down south.

He replied in the affirmative and affected a similar accent. "You Maria?"

The girl did not flinch. "You're Jack. I've seen you before. Yep, you can call me Maria. Sorry I couldn't make it over here till now. Life is not straightforward."

"It certainly isn't. When did we meet?"

"We didn't. It was a bit dark."

"Never mind, then. How can I help, Maria? I've been praying for you. For so long now."

Maria smirked. "Did my father ask you to do that? Don't believe a word of it. Let me tell you, I haven't had anything to do with him since they sent him down. He's never been in touch, never showed even a flicker of interest. I've nothing but contempt for the man."

"If it's any consolation, I chose to pray for you. I believe God can help us if we ask, and I have asked him to help you."

"That's weird, but I'm strangely pleased. I'd never have thought I'd say that. Yes, maybe God can." Maria smiled.

Jack was reassuring. "You see, prayer works! I've heard no more from him since the request he sent. But come on, if you dislike him that much, why are you here?"

She rubbed her eyes. "I could use a coffee."

Jack obliged. Dot brought it over and Jack did the introductions. Maria acknowledged her with a minimal hand gesture. Jack offered her a seat.

"Can't stop, Jack, too much to do." She looked at his guest. "But we'll have a chat soon, I'm sure." She returned to the kitchen with a fresh spring in her stride.

Maria pointed towards Dot's disappearing silhouette. "You told me in your message that my dad was here a few times. Was she around then?"

"She would have been, yes. Why?"

"No reason. I suppose she might remember him. But this isn't his sort of place, it really isn't. I don't see him being anywhere near anything Christian."

"It was a popular event, Maria. It was what we call an outreach event. Free food and real hope. There were lots of new people here. But remember him, yes, she might. So what's this about? Why did it take you so long to reply to my message? It's been ages."

"I'll be blunt. I'm fighting an addiction. I've been in rehab,

~ 24 ~

but still need support. I googled this place and when I saw what you do, I thought you would help me."

Jack smiled. "I'm maybe not the person you need. I'm an undertaker."

Maria forced a smile before Jack continued. "I do worship here, but we'll need to get Dot back over. She'll have the links you need to move you forwards."

"That's not all. I've run out of money. I don't want to seem crude, but I've had to fund my habit by providing sexual favours to the dealers, but they're getting more and more demanding and I've no choice but to comply. I'm scared, Jack. I'm in a trap. Now they're trying to get me to sell the stuff myself. I've refused. I've been threatened with a knife. I just hope one of them doesn't kill me."

Jack stared at her. "We're not talking cannabis, I guess."

"No. It's smack. The hard stuff. Heroin. I started on pot when my dad went missing from my life, and it's gone downhill since then."

"Listen, Maria, this must have been tough for you. Thanks for being honest. Give me twenty-four hours to ask some questions. I'd like to share your situation with Dot if you don't mind, especially that you might be looking to find God. Come back tomorrow, early afternoon."

Maria looked him full in the face. "You can ask Dot. I'll try to make that. If I don't show, it's because I can't." She looked around nervously before rising to her feet. "I've got to go now."

"Maria, I'll be praying for you tonight." He watched her leave, his face a picture of vague bewilderment and mild concern.

CHAPTER 3

The next day, it was Dot's turn to look around anxiously. "She won't show up, Jack. And even if she does, how do we know what she tells us is the truth?"

He checked his mobile and found an incoming message from his boss. "I've got to leave in a few minutes, I'm needed urgently at work. Maybe she's on her way, just delayed. I hope she gets here. If she doesn't, I'll be dreading what might have happened to her."

Dot's face brightened. "Why don't you leave her to me? She knows you've been praying. The rest is what I can do, woman to woman. You get to work." Her voice brimmed with confidence.

Jack smiled weakly. "I'll take that, Dot. Thanks. In my business, the trade keeps on coming, and I can't afford to lose any more working time over Maria. I guess we are all busy." A tinge of regret crossed his mind as he left, but he wasn't sure why.

The incoming mop of blue hair was tinged with light reflecting from the clear glass in the Hub door as it was pushed open. The visitor was greeted immediately and energetically. "Maria, good to see you. My name's Dot, if you don't remember. Take a seat."

The woman did as she was bid before glancing around the room. "I remember your name. Where's Jack?"

"Working. He sends his best. He's going to carry on praying for you. He's told me the story. You're in a bit of a pit, I guess."

"I am. Each time I climb one hill, I find a mountain behind it."

The mixed metaphors washed over Dot's head. "Right. I know that feeling, Maria. You're not alone, although your circumstances are pretty extreme, I have to say."

"I've made progress."

"I've made a few enquiries for you. We can get the authorities on your case and leverage on their resources."

Maria flinched. "What? That sounds painful."

Dot apologised. "Sorry, I mean get them to help you. We know the right people."

Maria stood up and raised her voice. "They're exactly the wrong people. It's not what they do that I don't get, it's why you think they would help me."

Dot motioned her enthusiastically to sit down. Maria sighed before complying. "Dot, I've been involved in an international hard illicit drugs supply chain. They're not exactly going to believe my story, are they?"

"I don't mean the police, Maria."

"They're all linked. They work together. No way can I go down that route. They'll have me banged up like they did with my father. He's to blame for all this in the first place."

"By deserting you?" Dot's tone was one of sympathy.

Maria's wasn't. "He introduced me to his so-called colleagues and friends. One in particular took a special interest in me, and I was flattered. I was impressionable, if you like. I know that now but didn't know it back then. It was grooming."

Dot's expression turned to shock. "Didn't your father see what was happening? Didn't he do anything?"

"He couldn't. By the time the grooming turned to exploitation, he was locked up and I was on my own. I was eighteen. The drugs came first, then the sex wasn't far behind. Then his mates got invited."

"What about your mother, Maria?"

"She left him years ago. She abandoned me with him."

"Abuse?"

"Not physical, but she got into a habit like me. She was out of control. She wasn't fit to be a mother once that started. Actually, I'm not sure whether she abandoned us, or my father made her go to protect me."

"Maybe she left to try to break the habit? As a child, you wouldn't have known, would you?"

"Dot, she left. That's enough for me."

"So if you could start a new life in another place, would that be something that would work for you?"

"I'd have to be safe, Dot. Another country. But I need some help here first. When I came here, I thought Jack could do that. I saw a story about what you do here. Oh, and I don't have much money."

"Ok. Listen, I'm in charge here, day to day. Leave that with me, if you will. In total confidence of course? I'll be the soul of discretion. That way you'll be as safe as possible."

"Ok. Great, Dot, so you should know that Maria isn't my

real name. I can't leave any traces of where I go in case they find me."

"Thank you for telling me. That will be totally between you and me. It's probably best if you don't come back here for a while, but we will keep in touch. Jack has the means of contacting you, I think."

"Yes, we could message each other via him. He seems like a good man."

Dot's face tensed. "Jack is, but actually, do you mind if we leave him out of it? I'd prefer to work with you. I'll give you my mobile number. He's a busy man."

"So I'm called Maria as far as he's concerned. Is that right, Dot?"

"Right."

Maria stood up. "And you call me that too."

Moments later, Dot was staring at an empty chair as the Hub door closed and Maria set off down the street. Dot loved a drama, and here was a real-life script. And for once she wasn't in the wings or front of house. She was an actor on the stage.

The following day, Jack looked up from the limousine he was polishing to see the unmistakeable bustle of Dot striding vigorously towards him.

"What are you doing here, Dot? Shouldn't you be at the Hub? Something wrong? I was coming over to see you anyway when I've finished."

"Update on Maria. I've agreed confidentiality with her. I said you'd be fine with that. Can't say more, other than she's leaving it with me."

Jack frowned. "That's not what I was hoping for. I'd forgotten that her father had requested confidentiality. I shouldn't have involved you, Dot. But if she agreed to that, I have no choice at this point."

Dot was ebullient. "You haven't. Trust me, Jack."

"I don't suppose you can tell her the Zac story?"

She shook her head. "There's a lot to sort out practically, Jack. That's the priority."

Jack looked downcast. "Shame you think that. I hope you haven't taken on too much here, Dot. The other day you were busy telling me how heavy your workload was, and here you are taking on what could be a wagon-load of someone else's problems."

Dot lowered her voice. "Leave it, Jack. Let's go with a woman's intuition and some out-of-the-box thinking. There may be a way of solving a lot of issues here." Before he could question her further, she had turned on her heels and was gone.

Jack shrugged and watched her reflection as it marched off in the direction of the Hub. As he picked up the chamois to finish his task, he couldn't help but feel that an opportunity was being missed.

That evening, Pete caught up with Jack ahead of an evening prayer meeting at the Hub.

"You haven't forgotten I'm on leave for ten days, Jack? It was arranged a while ago."

"No, I'm on it, Pete. Dot's not joining us tonight, by the way."

"I thought she wouldn't. I spoke to her earlier. She said she had too much on. Shame."

"She has, to be fair. We'll pray for her tonight, Pete."

"She mentioned that you've got a god-daughter, Jack. You kept that one in the dark, my friend! Shall we pray for her tonight too? Dot says you've asked her to get involved in helping the poor girl."

"Not strictly true, Pete. She's taken this one off my hands."

Pete tutted. "Oh dear. Not good. Dot's very practical, though, so she might surprise us both. If only she was a believer. We will pray for the situation. As you know, God can work through anyone, even those who are not of the faith. What's the story with Maria?"

"I had a text message from an unknown mobile number asking me to help her. It didn't say why, or how. There was an email address. The sender didn't give a name but said he was at the outreach mission we ran all those months ago and had my number from that."

"Ah, you mean 'Winner Winner'? The one with chicken dinner?"

Jack laughed. "Indeed. There's still a few success stories from that on our Hub website."

Pete smiled briefly before assuming a puzzled expression. "So what's the problem? You met up with her, right?"

"It's threefold, Pete. Firstly, she's got into a mess. Drugs. She needs support, but nothing involving the police. It's complex."

"Ok. What's second?"

"It was supposed to be totally confidential. But Dot has got involved and she's taken it over."

"Dot's very sensitive to people's needs, Jack, and she knows how to arrange help. What's third?"

"Don't know exactly. There's something that doesn't add up. She's from down south for starters."

Pete smirked. "You can't hold that against her, Jack."

"Ok. But I'm not sure that Maria is her real name. She told me I could call her that."

"Just an expression, Jack. Don't over-analyse. Is that it?"

"So I get a text from a number I don't know. There's no name, just the request and the email address I'd need. And it's supposed to be confidential. But when she rocks up to meet with me, she tells me she hasn't spoken to her father for years and has no respect and no relationship with him."

Pete's expression changed to something more defensive. "Where's this going, Jack? Some people are very wary of electronic communication and go anonymous."

Jack tapped the table three times. "How did the sender of the text have his daughter's email address if they haven't spoken for years? And why should he want to help her if she's cut him off for such a long time?"

Pete relaxed. "It could be a long shot, like an old email address from years ago. Jack, trust me, you're worrying over nothing. It'll all come out in due course."

Jack sighed. "When I read the text message, it didn't feel like a long shot. I hope we're not getting caught up in a clever scam. I so wish old Hamish was around."

Pete picked up his friend's concern. "Retired detectives like Hamish work on fading memories of how things are done, however willing they might be to help. Scams are present day issues, so I doubt if he'd been able to help. Anyway, he lives over two hundred miles away, in Surrey, so he's not likely to drop in."

"He's very reassuring to have around though. He was here for the outreach week when Dot was taken in by those heir hunters. I like the guy."

"Even though we don't know his real name? You gave him a nickname and we never got past that. Jack, you'd be suspicious of him now if it hadn't been you who'd started all this!"

Jack remained serious. "Probably. But we have a challenge, Pete, and a problem which I've caused."

Pete acknowledged his point. "Jack, look, I'll speak to Dot before I go and see what she's intending to do. You're right, we don't want her hurt, and we can't put the Hub at risk if it is something questionable."

Jack shook his head. "It's now totally confidential between her and Maria. I'm locked out of it. Dot won't give anything away."

Pete's expression turned to solemn. "In that case, we need to proceed carefully. We don't want any nasty surprises. Take it easy, Jack, it's probably nothing like what you're imagining. We've got our prayer meeting to worry about first."

"What's our theme tonight, Pete?"

"Luke 10, the Good Samaritan. It's funny how often the Bible speaks into a situation. It's about being good neighbours."

Jack nodded. "I know the story."

Pete clicked his fingers. "Tell me it in everyday language."

Jack looked puzzled. "Ok. Travellers on the road from Jerusalem to Jericho were so vulnerable to being attacked that even the rottweilers went round in pairs. This guy was a victim, beaten up, robbed and left for dead. Then the priest went past and ignored him, and so did a high-ranking cleric. The one who went to help was the most unlikely, a man from a country at odds with the Jewish people."

"Great. If you do that when everyone's here, I can help us see where we fit into that story." Pete pointed firmly at his Bible.

"Maybe Maria, or whoever she is, is the victim we're walking past, Pete. Are we sure Dot can provide what she requires? Maria needs the certainty of real hope. She needs physical and mental healing and help to see where she fits in God's creation. Dot can only stick a plaster on."

Pete put his hands together. "If Maria is telling the truth. Let's pray for guidance and wisdom this evening. Remember God speaks through his word. It'll all be fine. Let it rest."

"Even while you're away?"

"Especially while I'm away."

CHAPTER 4

Brittany's Pink Granite Coast had been a favourite haunt of Pete's for many years. Originally his mother's destination of choice for the family's annual holiday, at this stage of life Perros-Guirec offered him the peace and contemplation he needed after stepping back from full time work. Once there, he could rediscover memories aplenty from the locations they all loved, revisiting each one faithfully. Two calm overnight sea crossings on the Portsmouth to St Malo route had compensated for the stressful motorway journeys in England, and batteries recharged, he was returning to semi-retired UK life with a renewed vigour. His first day back found him heading across the meeting room at the Hub to his small office near the kitchen. His mind drifted briefly to the final evening's seafood platter served with a chilled Muscadet in a waterside restaurant near his favourite clifftop walk, before he was dragged out of his reverie by a voice he knew only too well.

"Unbelievable!" Dot blinked twice before staring fixedly at the screen of her smartphone. "I never win anything! This is worth thousands!"

Her new-found bounce struck Pete. Hearing Dot's less than melodious tones brought him back to reality with a jolt.

It wasn't that he hadn't seen Dot in this mood before, and it had sometimes ended in tears. He decided to sidestep her opening shot and rolled his eyes in jest before summoning up a cheery greeting. "Morning! You're looking bright! Busy day ahead?"

The reply was effusive. "I hope you enjoyed your break. It's always busy, Pete, managing this place. But it's so worth it. Real issues to deal with, real people to help. Oh, if you didn't hear me a moment ago, I've just won a holiday! All in! Free!"

Pete knew that, to her, disposable income was not a concept born of familiarity. Times appeared always hard for the divorcee. He smoothed back his thinning hair and attempted to calm her excitement. "Really? It would do you good. You haven't taken a break in all the time you've been with us, have you? I didn't know you did competitions, Dot. That's amazing news."

"To be honest, Pete, I don't recall entering one. I must have clicked something on the mobile by accident. But look, a week in somewhere called Sevilla!"

"Sevilla? Spelt with an 'a' on the end, not an 'e'? Might have originated in Spain, not the UK. Let me see that, Dot."

"Don't tell me it's a scam. That would be so cruel."

Pete scrolled down the screen before wincing slightly. "It's not just the spelling, Dot. Have you looked at the details? It's got fixed dates."

"Is that odd? Why? It's a prize."

"In two weeks' time." Pete drew a deep breath. "You'd

think they'd give you a bit of notice and a bit of choice, even for a prize."

"Can't you give me the time off? I haven't booked my holiday dates, mostly because I haven't got any planned. And as Jack would say, I'm skint."

Pete's face assumed a paternal expression. "Let's go one step at a time, Dot. You do have a history of over-excitement resulting from what some might see as financial opportunism. So far no money has ever materialised."

Dot frowned. "Don't underestimate me. Look, Jack told me a story about a zoo while you were away. He was talking about how to see things for what they really are."

A vision of a gorilla flashed through her head. Pete thought he heard a stifled snigger, which he ignored. "Just promise me you didn't click on anything or give your bank details."

Dot relented. "I'm not that soft, Pete, but thanks for being concerned. I presume you have never really trained a monkey." She laughed.

Pete shrugged. smiled politely and ignored the remark. "Fine. Forward me the details of this offer. I'll check it out for you. And run it by Jack. We don't want you hurt again."

Dot pursed her lips. "I learned a lot from the past, Pete. The business with our friend Sid a year or more ago, and the bogus heir hunters taught me the hard way. I don't take people at face value anymore. Not that Sid was a bad man. He'd become an honest, sincere citizen, albeit with a dodgy past."

"Criminal, Dot, criminal. Yes, Sid saw the light when he was here. The Lord changed him. Not everyone's like that, Dot. Use a bit of caution and common sense."

"This one feels genuine, Pete. I'm certain. The thing is that with this prize, if it is one, time's not on my side. It's in a fortnight. Where is this place anyway?"

Pete realised Dot was not for waiting. "Forward me it anyway, but look, it's a beautiful city in the south of Spain. Great place for theatre lovers like you."

Dot nodded enthusiastically. "With a decent beach?"

Pete bit his lip. Dot's notion of a good holiday was on a figurative collision course with his own. "Bit of a train ride to the sea, I'd say. Lots of great food though, and plenty of sun."

She resisted the urge to ask Pete if they grew bananas there. Jack's gorilla trainer of the same name seemed etched onto her brain. "Pete, I'll take it. Jack's due in later this morning."

Dot didn't have to wait that long. The door was opening as she finished the sentence, "Talking about me? What's this?" Jack adjusted his waistcoat and tie in a single movement and strode confidently into the room.

Her features betrayed relief. "I've won a holiday. Pete says it might be a scam. Will you look at it with him now?"

"I'm due in work shortly. It's a tough one so I called here for some inspiration. And a cup of your finest coffee, Dot. I'll come straight back when it's over. Can't get my head round anything else right now."

Pete raised an eyebrow. "What's the job, Jack? You've seen most scenarios in the undertaking business by now, so what's this one got?"

"It's a drug dealer. They say she got what was coming to her, but she did some terrible things. We're doing the requested embalming shortly, but the body carries the scars."

"Young woman?"

"Yes, 22. Whole life in front of her. Got hooked on heroin, ruined it."

"Tragic, Jack. You feel sorry for her, right?"

"You're joking, Pete, no. That girl ruined the lives of so many decent young people. It's them I'm sad for. I knew a few of them from where I live. Anyway, she killed herself before someone did it for her. I'd have been in the queue with them if I'd had the chance. Scum of the earth."

Dot emitted a low whistle. "I've never known you like this, Jack. How do her friends and relatives seem?"

"The ones I've met don't seem that bothered. There's an English bloke who lives in Spain come over to oversee things. He's very matter of fact, which doesn't seem right. He asked if I knew a man called Shaun who lived in Spain. I don't know anyone out there. It was an odd question to ask an undertaker. I'll be glad when this business gets to the cremation."

"Death makes people act strangely. All this seems to have made you furious, Jack." Dot seemed sympathetic.

"Dot, meeting Maria, even so briefly, after being asked to pray for her by her father has brought home to me the damage these evil people do. Maria was hooked by people like her. She might have been involved, who knows? There was a catalogue of stuff they never caught this woman for."

"You mustn't do the funeral if you're angry, Jack. It wouldn't be right." Dot's face was set.

"I'm a pro, Dot. I'll do the best job. And it's not anger that I'm fighting. It's the need for revenge. I know I shouldn't as a Christian, but I'm imagining the victim's face as an innocent child, not what heroin changed her into. Humans are so capable of terrible evil."

Pete smiled gently as Dot passed the requested coffee to Jack. "Get the embalming done well, Jack. It'll be good to talk of holidays when you've got the task over. And make sure you do a top job, my friend."

CHAPTER 5

"How did it go? Are you ok?" Dot was alone in the Hub. She'd been watching for Jack's car.

"All done, Dot. We'd made her beautiful. Sickeningly beautiful. Have you made any progress with Maria?"

Dot evaded the question. "Some days I feel proud to know you, Jack, and this is one of them. Your good friend Sid would say the same."

"I miss him, Dot. One of those you don't easily forget. Especially the trips to the pub when he was with us."

Dot's look turned to wistful. "I often wonder where he is and what he's up to."

Jack briefly wondered if she knew, but he nodded. "You know, Dot, he had a soft spot for you, and it wasn't a bog at the bottom of his garden." He had rediscovered his mojo.

Dot grinned broadly for the first time that morning. "You don't mean an outside lavatory, I take it. Yes, I have missed our Sidney, or whatever his real name might have been. It'd be hard to know him as anything other than Sid. I can't believe he was ever a con man."

Jack's glance was swift but affirming. "Don't worry about

his real name, he'll answer to Sid. He'll be living under a new identity, for sure, as he still has enemies in high places. One thing is for sure, Dot, he'll be a new man. He received forgiveness from God for all his past crimes, so he will be experiencing a new kind of real freedom. Rather like Zaccheus."

"Really?" Dot was unconvinced. "To me he was a loveable rogue. Sid, not Zaccheus. I just wish he would walk back through the door here, Jack."

"That's not going to happen, Dot. His past caught up with him. There was a bullet with his name on it if he'd stayed put."

"I know. You tell me God reached out to him when he was in the nick. I'd like to believe it's true, but I just can't."

"He'd done wrong, Dot. He'd damaged a lot of people. He'd made enemies for life."

"So if he wasn't a loveable rogue, why would this God of yours want to bother with him?"

"Well, why did Jesus bother with Zaccheus? Forgiveness gave him a new confidence. In my opinion, finding God gave Sid a thirst for truth, and that's what you saw in him. He's in transition, if you like. I believe he is responding to God's unconditional love, one day at a time."

"I'd love to think that's true, Jack. It seems too easy."

"It wasn't easy for Jesus, Dot. Think of it this way. Sid has been freed from his past. It's like it never happened. That's so amazing that it takes a long time to fully understand it. Try and see it from his point of view."

"I do, Jack. I do. But if he was so evil that there's a contract out on his life, I still don't get why your God is interested in him in the first place."

"Maybe God is working through him to reach out to others, Dot."

"Would he do that? Would he? When there are so many holier people around?"

"There's no such thing, Dot. Every one of us does wrong. Humans fall short, all of us. Let me put the situation in your terms, though."

"Go on, Jack. I'm all ears."

"Listen, he opened his heart to me on more than one occasion. He was genuinely fond of you. This story is not over. He had some personal issues to resolve which would take time. My gut feeling – and that's all it is, Dot – tells me there's a new chapter to be written for the two of you. I don't think he wanted you to get hurt when he was with us for those few weeks."

"Everyone's so protective round here." Dot's tone was one of slight irritation.

"He'll share his new freedom with you, Dot, if I'm right. No guilt, no blame. And no cost to you. It's all been paid for by Jesus Christ."

"Are you applying that to the woman you just embalmed, Jack?"

"I would if I knew she'd repented, Dot. It's hard to believe."

"Like this holiday I've won. Pete is so suspicious. There's really no need. I won, that's all. Why does he have to be like that?"

"Dot, it's advice, that's all. Always listen to the views of those you trust."

Jack looked up and grinned at the figure who had just walked in. "Your ears were burning, were they not?"

Pete took a seat and surmised accurately. "The Spain holiday, right? Looking at Dot, I guess she needs a break after listening to you, my friend."

Jack acknowledged the lightening of the conversation. "Me too. Did I tell you about the time we embalmed the Squirrel?"

"I'm guessing a career burglar who hoarded all his ill-gotten gains?" Dot shrugged her shoulders.

Jack raised a finger in denial. "He was 6 foot 10. Loved cashews and pistachios. Ate them all his life. His long-suffering estranged wife disliked him with a vengeance. She made one unusual request."

Pete wondered briefly where Jack was heading before asking the question anyway. "I know I'm going to regret this, but what was it?"

"Normal beds were too small. He used to curl up like a squirrel whenever he lay down to sleep. That's where his nickname came from. The wife, who didn't want to pay for a bigger casket, gave us written instructions to put him in the position in which he slept."

Pete's relief was short-lived. "Sounds reasonable to me."

Jack was not for stopping. "No, there's more. She wanted the packet of what he was eating when he died to be placed by the lower part of his face in the standard dimension coffin. She wrote that it was a wish which originated from the early days of their marriage."

Pete became perplexed. "What on earth had she written?"

Dot spoiled the tale. "I've heard this one before. She'd wanted to see his nuts squashed under his chin. What's the news on the holiday scam, Pete? If I didn't need one before hearing that story again, I do now."

Jack opened his arms in apology. "What have you found, Pete?"

Pete clasped his hands together before placing them on his knees. "Dot, are you sure you didn't enter a competition of some sort? I've checked it all out, it's definitely odd, but I can't see it being a scam."

Dot affected amazement. "No way! Great! Where's it come from then?"

"It seems to be from an email address of a person who works in tourism. It's personal, not from an organisation. I've run a check."

Jack moved his arms to a folded position. "A freelancer, Pete. Is that what you're saying?"

"Probably, Jack. The hotel looks to be in private ownership, so it might be a promotion for them. It's a decent place, by the look of the website."

"So what are you advising Dot, Pete?"

"Caution is the watchword, don't build your hopes up yet, but with one further issue to mention, I'd say Dot can book those dates off work."

Dot moved across to hug her two friends as they rose from their chairs. Pete obliged immediately, but Jack hung back. "What's the remaining matter, Pete?"

"It's the prize. Flights, accommodation, dinner, bed and breakfast."

Jack contorted his face slightly. "Sounds spot on. Only bettered by a free bar, in my view."

Pete smiled. "That's not it. It isn't for one or even two persons. It's for three, all in single rooms."

"Are you sure? That is a bit weird, Pete."

"It's all there, Jack. Maybe the hotel had a rush on bookings, and it was all they had left."

Dot had little time for the finer points. She had a Spanish holiday to plan. It was left to Pete to raise the final question. "Who are you taking with you, Dot? You should definitely not go alone."

"Not sure, Pete. I thought of some of my friends and family when I got the notification today, but it will be too short notice for them. And most of my other friends are here at work."

"Just a tip, Dot, but you'll probably need to get that sorted tonight if not beforehand. Look, I think you should put Jack and me on the guest list with you. If it is risky, we'll be there for you."

Dot sniffed. "You seem very sure. What about the Hub? We can't all just waltz off."

Pete had thought of that. "I sorted it earlier. A couple of our older members who will step in. They know the routines. He's a retired chef and she did front of house in his restaurant."

Dot sniffed more loudly. "I hope I'll still have a job when I get back. Are you certain this is such a good idea?"

Jack narrowed his eyes and looked her full in the face. "We are, Dot, we really are."

CHAPTER 6

The Guadalquivir shimmered gently in the cool pre-breakfast sunshine as Jack turned back towards the hotel. The mercury began its inexorable climb towards the high thirties as he looked across Triana bridge towards Seville's historic centre, causing his thoughts to return to the air conditioning unit which had given him such a good night's sleep. The flight had seemed long to him, with a phlegmatic Pete and an excited Dot alongside.

Jack didn't do hot. The stopping train up from Malaga had not been without its challenges, but an open window had allowed waves of scented olive grove air to blow across their table. The knotted handkerchief option had remained in his pocket.

He made his way through the lobby, studiously avoiding all risks of a gaze from any receptionist. A furtive glance showed that he needn't have worried. There was no-one there to even launch a friendly 'hola' in his direction. Jack's Spanish knowledge began and ended with this word. He knew deploying it too earnestly might bring a more complex reply which was beyond his grasp.

Pete, who knew less of the language than he did of French, was waiting for Dot outside the breakfast room door. Dot was now ten minutes late for the agreed meeting time of 8.30 am, so Pete motioned to Jack to lead the way in.

Jack shook his head and returned the gesture with a shrug. He turned his attention to the floor and studied it intently to avoid an unsolicited linguistic approach from a welcoming waiter. Pete shrugged his shoulders in response and led the way to a window table for four with a view onto the hotel garden, where the patio seats were all taken. Pete placed his jacket on a third chair to reserve it and, moments later, Dot turned up and sat on the fourth one, blissfully unaware of Pete's attempt at early morning gallantry.

"Whose is this jacket? Morning Pete. Morning Jack. Turned out nice, I see."

"Mine. Beautiful out there." Pete gestured towards the garden as he retrieved his garment. "If we're up early enough tomorrow, we'll take that option. Do you want me to order breakfast for you?"

"Coffee please. And some fruit salad. Those oranges look gorgeous." Dot surveyed the remainder of the buffet. "Do we help ourselves?"

A voice behind her made her jump. "Yes of course, my dear Señora. Please. Coffee for three?" The waiter raised his eyebrows in anticipation of an order.

Jack's relief was plain at hearing his native tongue. He began to babble. "Ah, you speak English. Yes to the coffee. Never drink the tea abroad. And why do you call her Senyora? Her name's Dot. And we serve ourselves at the buffet?"

The waiter didn't flinch. "Even in Spain, yes. I guess you no speak Spanish?"

Jack shook his head firmly. "No, I only speak two languages. English and gibberish." He peered at the waiter's name badge. "Pedro. I'm Jack."

Pedro bowed. "Happy to meet you, sir. Señora is not Spanish first name. In English you say Madam, but we are in Spain! Maybe I help you speak a little Spanish before your stay finish."

Jack grimaced and pointed to his companion. "This is Pete. Try him."

It was Pete's turn to bow. "Pedro. Same name as mine. Good to meet you."

Pedro laughed. "Okay, hello Jack, hello Pete, hello Dot. You need anything, you ask me. But Jack, I set you a challenge. Tomorrow you must wish me 'good morning' in Spanish. You learn it from the lady on reception, perhaps? She very nice."

Pete's eyes shone. "We'll see to it, Pedro. Are you local?"

The waiter hesitated. "Loco? Me? Mad?"

Pete turned the colour of the Rioja on the wine counter, but Pedro pre-empted his apology. "I joke. Local, yes, from this region. You are tourists, yes?"

Dot sniffed. "Not exactly, Pedro. We're competition winners. I won this holiday."

Pedro clicked his fingers. "You. I know of this. Is arranged by hotel."

Dot failed to restrain a grin. "There you go, Pete. Not half board or full board, but above board."

Pedro checked his phone. "Today is Alcazar. Royal palace. You have tickets at hotel reception. Special guests."

Dot's look turned to surprise. "I don't recall entrances being included. That's amazing!"

Pete said nothing. Jack gave Dot a thumbs up and turned to the waiter. "How do we get there from here?"

It was Dot who answered the question. "In a taxi. I'm sure Pedro will get us one."

Pedro wasn't so sure. "Jack should tell the señora on reception in Spanish when you ready. She is Marina."

Jack smirked. "Did her parents own a few yachts?"

Pedro stifled a smile before adopting a blank look. "Marina speak English and Spanish too. She help. Hotel take care of taxi bill." Only then did he grin at Dot and headed out of the room.

Ten minutes later, Pedro was back, this time looking slightly flushed. Jack scraped his chair backwards across the polished floor tiles and placed his serviette on his plate. "Don't let them take it. I haven't finished yet."

He headed to the lobby, where he was anticipating a brief conversation with Señora Marina. He was disappointed. The abandoned blue castored chair was all that greeted him. He tapped on the desk in hope of attention.

He got some. The chef rushed past him towards the stairs, spurning the wait for a lift. "No here, sorry," he blurted, "urgency up." He gestured towards the floors above and was gone. Jack picked up a solitary leaflet advertising the Alcazar and wandered back to his breakfast. A smart side-step befitting a man of younger years than the English undertaker averted a damaging collision with Pedro, who was hot on the tracks of the chef.

Pete was deep in conversation with Dot when Jack returned

to his seat. He broke off briefly. "Any joy with a taxi? Got the tickets? Did she teach you the Spanish for taxi?"

Jack shook his head and shrugged. "She wasn't there. I got a leaflet about that place we're visiting. I'll try in a few minutes. In English. There's something happened upstairs. They're all sorting it out."

Pete refocussed on Dot, who smiled at Jack apologetically. She hijacked his account of Perros-Guirec to briefly talk family. "I wish I'd met your mum, Pete. She sounds a remarkable lady. Overcoming all the difficulties of her past, setting up the group that became the Hub, she'd be so proud of you now. And everything you've done."

Pete wasn't convinced. "I see you brought your rosy specs. You know the issues we've coped with. Bad ones. Including the murder of one of our own. And is there a right way of dealing with child abuse? I don't think pride is the word, Dot."

Dot's colour drained. "Sorry, Pete. The murder got to me as much as anyone. Not that I knew that man, but he was one of your friends. I don't know how you coped."

It was Pete's turn to shrug. "Faith helps, Dot, that's all. That man, as you call him, had turned to God after committing some unspeakable crimes against his own daughter when she was a child. God forgives anyone and anything if they turn to him with sincerity. He's in glory now, Dot."

She emitted a deep sigh. "Why doesn't your God just stop it happening, Pete?"

Pete managed a weak smile. "We don't have God's perspective as humans, Dot. He is with us in everything, though, and walks with us during our time on his earth. You just have to look for him."

Jack had been listening intently. Now he joined the conversation. "He does that. I've been at the back of more funerals than most. Some are unbelievably sad, and some are so hollow. But some speak of light, and hope, like death isn't the end of life. And I don't think a God who created this world would mess up on his creation. Growing old, suffering pain, sickness and then dying only makes sense if there's more to it. Right, Pete?"

Pete's reply was cut short by the siren of an approaching ambulance. He smiled at the irony. "Evil is a sickness in the heart of every person. We want to do things our way, not God's. Then we complain to God that it has gone wrong."

Jack sniffed. "I used to like it when they played 'My Way' at funerals. I like a bit of Sinatra, always have. But not at the crem. It's rather sad that people think it's even appropriate. It seems to me that they sing it to celebrate rebellion, you know, ignoring God's way."

Dot's perplexed look softened to one of mere puzzlement. "That's a bit deep for this time of day. I wonder what's going on upstairs. Is that ambulance outside? I could do with getting back to my room. We've got a palace to visit."

She had hardly finished her words when a figure bearing a suitcase came through the door, put the case down by a vacant table for two and made to pour a coffee from the flask on the buffet. Jack nudged Pete. "Looks like a Spanish version of Hamish to me."

Dot shot the newcomer a quick glance. "The retired detective guy from Surrey who was around the group when Sid was about? He does!"

Pete drew a sharp intake of breath. "It's him!"

Jack did likewise before Pete nodded. "Remember his name isn't Hamish. Jack called him that when we first got to know him, and it stuck. If it's not him, I'm a Dutchman."

The focus of their conversation sipped his coffee and put the white beaker back on its saucer. "Anyone speak English? I can't find anyone on reception." His eyes toured the room and alighted on Jack. "Is that you, my friend? And Pete? And a lady whose name escapes me. I had a feeling I might find you lot."

"Hamish!" Jack was first to reply. "It is you! What on earth are you doing here?"

"I'm on holiday. You too, I guess. It is a small world, isn't it? Forgive me, but I rather had you all down as beach bums, not creatures of culture in a place like Seville."

Jack grinned at Dot. "Hamish, let me move Pete's jacket. You sit here."

Hamish accepted and moved towards the vacant chair but stumbled over Dot's handbag which was in the way. His coffee spilled onto the seat as he hung on to the beaker handle.

Jack passed his serviette over to Dot who safely channelled and cut off the dark flood which had been heading towards her trousers. "You're in luck, Hamish. That happened to my mate in a fast-food restaurant, but it was far worse."

"Dropped his coffee and it went all over his shirt?" Hamish ventured the notion nervously.

"No, worse. He slipped and sat down hard on his nuggets."

Hamish grinned. "Painful! Actually, I've always wondered which bit of a chicken that was."

Dot rolled her eyes and changed the subject. "Can we know

your real name? It doesn't seem right when everyone keeps calling you Hamish." She looked up at the new arrival.

"Hamish is fine. I've got used to it. They call me that at home now." He peered down his nose at Dot.

She acknowledged his comment before moving the conversation forward. "Do you speak Spanish, Hamish?"

He affected a sad face. "I'm afraid not. I was never any good at languages when I was at school. What about you, Jack? I have you down as a potential polyglot."

Jack sighed. "I've been called a few things in my life, but that's a new one. A polygon might be a dead parrot, but what on earth is a polyglot?"

Pete intervened. "Someone who speaks several languages. I don't think that's Jack, Hamish."

Jack's face showed mock relief. "Listen, I'm going to do some litter-pick walk linguistics while we're here. Pete."

"I know I'll regret asking this, but what's that, Jack?"

"I'll just pick the language up as I go along. It's the best way. I was made to learn French at school, but it was all grammar. The teacher wore a gown, it was that traditional. I was ok until I had trouble with my gerundives. Nasty."

Dot's expression became one of empathy. "Must have been really tough, Jack. Mind, things had changed by the time I was in full time education. For the better. We got to choose from three languages, including Spanish."

Hamish raised a hand. "Can you help me with my check-in, Dot? That'd be great."

Dot's head was already shaking. "I learned Spanish for two years and have forgotten it for about thirty. Pedro will sort you out."

Hamish was about to ask who Pedro was when the man himself, reddened and clearly flustered, marched back into the room. Pete's expression turned to one of concern.

Not so Jack, who decided that this was the moment to ease Hamish's linguistic embarrassment. "Pedro, come here. Here's a new amigo."

Hamish looked at Jack. "Amigo? You know more than you're letting on. Let's try another one. How do you say good morning in Spanish?"

Jack smirked. "I heard Pedro greet a guest earlier. Was it 'Buenos Aires'?"

Hamish opened his mouth before pulling a face. Jack, though, had moved on to Pedro. His fluency was unchained. "Who's rattled your cage, amigo?"

The waiter's face was resolutely red. "Upstairs is very bad. Accident. Much blood. Marina go hospital. Please you stay in restaurant."

Pete gestured helpfully towards the hotel garden and Pedro rushed off to inform the al fresco breakfasters before slamming the dining room door firmly shut.

Behind it, the lift brought a stretcher case to ground level and automatically pinged the door closed after the patient was carried to the waiting ambulance. No-one returned to the ample buffet to recharge their plates and beakers, or even collect a new serviette. Except Jack.

Dot broke into a quiet smile. She glanced at Pete. "He did say he hadn't finished yet."

CHAPTER 7

A full half hour passed before the guests were released back to their rooms. Jack was the only one of the four whose key indicated a fourth-floor location, and the inquisitive Dot insisted on accompanying him to his door. The scene around them was normal, apart from an aroma of carpet cleaner mingled with unscented bleach, coming from the maintenance store. She went down somewhat disappointed.

It was just before 11 am when they regrouped in the lobby. Pedro was becalmed in the unaccustomed and unwanted role of receptionist. Jack said nothing as his new Spanish friend was already calling the taxi with one hand whilst proffering the envelope with Alcazar entrance tickets for four in the other. Pete was sporting elegant shorts, whilst Hamish made his way out onto the street to spot the approach of their transport.

Dot's face was almost matriarchal. "I'm so glad I chose you two to come with me on this holiday. I have been known to do the odd daft thing in my life, but I feel very safe with you, Pete, and there's always something to smile at with you, Jack."

Two minutes later, Hamish re-entered the lobby. "It's here. El taxi, Jack. Let's go."

As they climbed into the car, Dot noted that Jack's trousers were turned up. He spotted her glance and grinned. "Mid-thirties today, Dot. It's a hot one."

She smiled back. "Be prepared, eh?"

Jack looked at Pete. "Seems they knew Hamish was joining us. Four tickets provided, not three. Curiouser and curiouser."

Just a few minutes later, they found themselves approaching the entrance to the Alcazar palace.

"You is English, no?" The uniformed official peered out through the perforated screen of his Alcazar kiosk, eyebrows raised. Pete seized the initiative.

"Four adults, we have tickets."

The official smiled at the implied answer to his rhetorical question but wasn't having it. "You is English, no? I need see tickets."

Dot pushed Pete aside and took over. "Yes love. We is English."

The man's grin disappeared. "You have Mr Dot?" He stared at her.

Pete realised the conversation was heading down a very short cul de sac and eased Dot firmly but gently back to the edge of the counter.

He took charge. "Why do you ask?"

The employee, grey haired and wizened by the Seville sun, waved a delaying finger and slid off his chair in the direction of the room behind. Seconds later, he was back. "En – vel – ope. I have for Mr Dot."

Pete caught sight of the front panel. Handwritten in capital letters, there were the three letters of her name. Nothing else. He moved the discussion on as his friend assumed a bewildered expression. "Yes, we have Mr Dot."

Pete extended his hand, anticipating receipt, but it didn't arrive. Instead, the man slid his finger down the flap and opened it, pulling out a piece of lined paper. He scanned it before passing it over. Pete made to move away, only to be met with another wagging finger. "Is from Mr Domingo. You read then you go in." He jabbed his thumb repeatedly towards the entrance, looked round and grabbed his phone. Clumsily, he began a text message.

Pete read the message in a deliberate fashion. It was in perfect English. He nodded to the official, who motioned them into the palace. They moved in the direction indicated before Dot stopped. "What was that all about, Pete?"

Hamish jumped in. "A mix-up over your gender, Dot. Nothing more."

Dot's features turned to relief, but Jack grabbed the letter. He was not satisfied yet and read aloud. "I'll see you later. I hope you enjoy Sevilla. Thank you for coming here. Look out for me after your visit."

Hamish spotted the warning signs on Jack's furrowed brow. "Jack, don't overthink this. There's probably some publicity for someone in our visit. After all, we won a competition. Prize winner shots are inevitable."

Jack was on it in a flash. "We won? Dot did, and she invited me and Pete. Are you saying she invited you?"

Hamish held up his hand. "No, not at all. But someone did. I got a similar message to Dot. I'd won. My flight was from London, though."

Dot was bewildered. "You won the same competition? Why didn't you tell us?"

Hamish looked sheepish. "I didn't want to burst your bubble, to be honest. I knew as soon as I saw you that this was no competition prize, but the detective in me needed to learn more. So I said nothing."

"So what is it?"

"If you read crime novels, Dot, you'd think it was some intrigue of international proportions, but in real life these things are fairly mundane."

"So what is it?" Dot's voice betrayed a growing impatience.

"I don't know yet, but it'll be fun watching what happens next. Someone is pulling our strings. Dot, do you still have those tv producer links from the Covid documentaries you were in, the ones about the Hub?"

"They are a bit like my childhood crush on Cliff Richard. He and I became penfriends for a while."

"That's amazing, Dot!"

She grinned. "I wrote regularly, but he never replied. Same with the producer contacts."

"Ah, ok, there could be a reason for that. It's some kind of retrospective on the pandemic community work you all did, the foodbank, the needs you met, the families you supported. Just sit back, relax, and look out for hidden cameras."

Dot's shoulders dropped. "Phew, wow. I'm so glad you're here, Hamish. I'd never have thought of that."

Jack was less than convinced. "So who is Mr Domingo? It can't be Placido. And did you notice the envelope this morning had four tickets in? Pedro said nothing about that. How did that happen?"

"Domingo is a common surname, Jack."

Jack shrugged. "This is all very odd. I'm not sure young Pedro is telling us everything he knows. I hope that this Mr Domingo will have the answers."

Hamish frowned. Dot put her hand on Jack's arm. "Maybe Hamish is wrong, Jack. Maybe it was part of the holiday package, Jack. I never read the small print."

Jack smirked and threw a swift glance at Hamish before fixing Dot with a stare. "That's fine with me, Mr Dot. Well, almost fine. We're on a holiday prize for a competition no-one entered, and Hamish rocks up as another victorious participant. But I'll buy the story for now. Let's go in before we get rumbled."

Dot shrugged, the visit began and two hours passed by. Pete and Hamish were fascinated. Dot asked a lot of questions. But history wasn't Jack's cup of tea, and his expression glazed over. He left the other three as they lingered lengthily over a particularly intricate ceramic tile and sat down, shaded from the sun by a souvenir stall to wait for them to complete their wall-covering inspection. His eyes began to close.

Moments later, his doze was interrupted by a voice.

"Mr Dot?" The kiosk man was back.

"Buenos Aires!" Jack's response came from a mix of surprise and somnolence.

The man rolled his eyes. "Dias, dias! I have second message for you Mr Dot. Mr Domingo say he no come, he contact you."

Jack closed his eyes pensively for a moment and drew a deep breath. "Who is Mr Domingo? What does he do?"

He looked up. The man had gone.

Twenty minutes later, the four tourists were relaxing over a drink close to the cathedral. Hamish, Pete and Dot were still enthusing over the Alcazar, but Jack's mind was elsewhere. He left them to it and wandered back to the hotel.

Pedro greeted him from behind the reception desk. Jack acknowledged him. "How's your colleague, Pedro?"

The waiter shook his head. "Not good, señor. Not good. A terrible accident."

Jack set his hands to a prayerful pose before accepting his key. "Pedro, tell me, do you know Mr Domingo?"

Jack thought he caught a look of terror briefly before the waiter composed himself. "Domingo? No, I don't think so. No."

Behind him, the lift door opened and a lady emerged before briskly heading to the exit. Lingering by the door was not on her agenda. Jack caught sight of her back as she left the building and was gone. This lady was not unfamiliar. He racked his brain but couldn't place her.

CHAPTER 8

"Sunday."

Dot brushed an imaginary hair from her face. "Why do you say that, Pete?"

"It's what Domingo means."

Jack arrived to join the breakfast conversation, fresh from his early morning constitutional. "Buenos Aires, amigos."

Pete ignored the greeting. "So it's a clue."

Dot raised one eyebrow. "Sunday. Mr Sunday. He might be a columnist in a newspaper."

Hamish scraped the fourth chair back along the floor as he joined the group, coffee tightly clasped. "We're on that again, are we?"

Jack nodded. "We are. Domingo means Sunday. Doesn't mean it has to be a clue as to the identity of our benefactor, does it?"

Their deliberations were interrupted by the sight of a police car slowing as it approached the hotel. A few minutes later, Pedro came over apologetically and pointed at Jack. "You come, please. Help police."

Jack frowned before acquiescing. It would be fully two

hours before he returned. When he did, he found his friends waiting in the bar.

Pete was first to speak. "Jack, where've you been?"

Jack sighed. "Seville main police station. Yesterday may not have been an accident. Our victim fell onto something sharp, but was she pushed?"

Pete's look turned to concern. "How's she doing?"

Jack shook his head sadly. "Not good. Her injuries are still life-threatening, or so they told me."

Hamish looked up. "How do you know? I thought you'd didn't do Spanish."

"One of them spoke some English."

"So why did they want you, my friend?" Hamish looked at Jack.

"My room is on the floor where it happened."

The retired detective shrugged. "So were a few other people."

Jack pulled a face. "I told them I was out for my morning walk when it probably happened. I stated that there was no-one on reception when I returned but said I didn't think that was odd at the time. I then went into the restaurant for breakfast. Then they said I had no alibi. Marina is in intensive care, and even she wasn't there to see me go out. Hamish, I'm a person of interest in a criminal event."

Hamish gestured to him to calm down. "Steady on, my friend. What else did you tell them?"

"They asked me about drugs. I told them about Maria and then the dealer we'd buried. I said how much I hated people who did evil. They know what my views are on that topic."

"Did you tell them what you do for a living?"

"Yes. I said undertaker. Then I made a few jokes, like telling them that I put most of my clients in a coffin. That was not a good idea, it seems."

"Did they know what an undertaker is?"

"How do I know, Hamish? Maybe not really."

"Jack, did you see anyone as you made your way to the lift for your walk?" Hamish's tone was quietly reassuring.

"No, but there were a few voices. I'd no idea what most of them were saying, of course. But I did hear two English speakers as well, from a room near mine. A man and a woman. I couldn't help listening as I passed. From the snippets I caught, I suspect that they'd not long arrived and were planning to skip breakfast to catch up on missed sleep."

Hamish nodded. "If I'm right, anyone on that floor will be giving statements this morning. Probably at the police station, with the interpreter guy. Let's hope they're not undertakers too." Hamish folded his arms. "Nothing to worry about, Jack, once the full picture emerges."

CHAPTER 9

"We've lost enough time. Let's head to the Cathedral first. It's rather special, I gather. Then why don't we try some tapas for a late lunch?" Pete was ready to go.

Hamish smiled gently. "If it's ok with Mr Domingo. Shall we assume he has no plans for us?"

"We shall." Pete's tone was firm. "Jack, can you use your command of Spanish to persuade Pedro to call us a taxi?"

Jack shook his head slowly. "I'm not coming with you. I need some time. You three go. Tell me about it later."

Dot's look turned to one of concern. "I'll stay with you, Jack, if you want."

"I wouldn't dream of it, Dot. You won this holiday and I'm not going to spoil it for you."

As the taxi pulled away, Jack waved and turned to head back to his room. The lift came down from the fourth floor to collect him. He stood back to allow the occupant to step out before entering the lift himself, but he didn't get that far.

"Is that you, Jack?" It was the lady he had glimpsed previously. "Remember me? It's Judy. We did your outreach week in Liverpool a year or two back."

"Judy! Of course. Do you still work in Paris? What on earth are you doing here? Is Roger with you? Don't tell me you both won a competition."

"Slow down, Jack. We lead a church in Brittany now. And Roger is here, it's just that he likes to walk down the stairs. He'll be here any moment. And what's this nonsense about a competition?"

"Nothing, Judy, just a silly joke. Here's Roger!"

"It's Jack, Roger. Jack from the Hub in Liverpool. You remember him, don't you?" Judy raised her eyebrows.

"Indeed I do. The undertaker. Good to see you. What are you doing here, Jack? Has the business expanded this far?"

Jack acknowledged the humour. "How long have you got?"

"Ah. You're staying here, right?"

"Right. Fourth floor. Same as you? How long have you been here?"

Roger nodded. "A couple of nights."

"We haven't seen you at breakfast, have we?"

"No. We're on room only. We do our own. Judy prefers that. Keeps the costs down for the person paying. And we love Seville from my student days, so we love the evenings in the city centre."

Judy raised a finger. "You said 'we', Jack. Who's with you? Pete, I guess. And the lady who ran the Hub?"

"Yup. Both of them. Remember the detective guy?"

"The one we called Hamish?"

"He's here too."

Roger looked perplexed. "No way! Is this some kind of therapy holiday? Jack, who was the guy the bullet was intended for? Wasn't he called Sid? Is he here too? I thought he'd made a run for it, to a safe haven."

"He did, Roger. Don't know where. And I'll take the idea of a week-long wake in Spain on board. I know a few customers back in the UK who would go for that."

"Ok, listen, Jack, we've got an appointment shortly at the police station. Shouldn't be too long."

"With an interpreter, Roger?"

"No need. I speak Spanish. My degree's in European languages. But listen, can we all do dinner tonight? I know a great place in town where the students used to hang out. The food's awesome. We'll meet here in the foyer at 8 pm."

Jack smiled. "I'm sure that'll be fine. We'll need a couple of taxis. I'll speak to Pedro."

"Taxis? No need. We'll go on shanks' pony. Get the steps in. I know the short cuts."

With that, they were gone. Jack rubbed his eyes in disbelief.

CHAPTER 10

"La cuenta, por favor." Roger put his finger and thumb together and rubbed them up and down until the waiter acknowledged him.

"I couldn't eat one of those, Roger, whatever you've ordered." Jack patted his stomach. "I'm tapassed out."

Pete smiled. "I was requesting the bill, Jack. But now you have a new word for your English vocabulary. And everyone else's!"

Dot too was replete. "Great food, Roger. How did you choose this place? I love it!"

Roger grinned. "I always go where the students eat. Quality and price in perfect harmony."

Judy wagged a finger. "Come on, Roger, you had a tip off, be honest. If it wasn't for Mr Domingo, we wouldn't be here."

Dot drew breath. "Mr Domingo? You've heard of him too?"

Judy opened the palms of her hand. "Of course. That's why we are here. He wants to meet with us."

Pete's brow furrowed. "For what purpose, may I ask?"

Before Judy could reply, the waiter came over. Pete translated. "No bill to pay. Mr…" He got no further.

"Domingo paid." It was Jack. "Hamish, what's happening? I'm struggling to believe all this hospitality. Something's going on."

Hamish produced a Gallic shrug. "Relax, Jack. Chill. Go on, Judy, why does Mr Domingo want a meeting with you?"

Roger supervened. "Hamish, we no longer work in Paris. We now work in a Breton church supported by a British mission charity. They began in Brittany over sixty years ago, setting up evangelical churches across France. The country was a huge holiday destination but a desert for biblical faith. The French people were in dire need, and we Brits were their neighbours. Good Samaritan stuff. We're back in the region where they began."

Judy refocused the conversation. "We had a message from Mr Domingo a few weeks ago. He explained that he wanted to explore setting up a church in Southern Spain. He invited us down for a planning meeting. Didn't Pete mention it? We asked him to put it on the Hub prayer e-mail."

Pete looked embarrassed. "I was saving it for next month, Judy. There's been so many people asking us to pray for them and their issues."

"No worries, Pete. Let's get back to our benefactor."

Roger nodded. "He offered to pay all our costs. He even offered a donation to our own church as he knew we couldn't just drop everything and head south. So we managed to get cover for a week, and here we are."

Hamish rubbed his chin. "Have you had any money yet?"

Roger waved a hand in the direction of the restaurant

reception. "He's thought of everything. We haven't paid a thing. Why do you ask?"

Hamish looked thoughtful. "Just building a picture of the man. Our experience has been similar. He's, erm, remarkably generous."

Dot sucked at her cheeks before staring at Pete. "My holiday theory is starting to look rather thin. What have I got us all into?"

Judy and Roger looked simultaneously quizzical. Pete raised an index finger. "That's why I insisted on Jack and I travelling with you, Dot. I knew there was more to this than met your eye."

Hamish was reassuring. "It's all good. We're still understanding things, but this is no con artist. We are all obviously significant in the mind of Mr Domingo, if nothing else. He's certainly investing in us. Now let's go back to the hotel."

CHAPTER 11

Breakfast the next morning was animated. As they finished, Pete pushed his coffee cup away and stood up. "Let's hit the day. Conference with Roger and Judy in the lobby, in ten minutes."

Dot nodded thoughtfully. "Let's see what Mr Domingo is planning to pay for today!"

Ten minutes later, they had gathered. Pedro approached the group with an air of importance.

He waited until Pete nodded in his direction. "Mr Domingo phone and say he come today. Here. In a few minutes. He want meet you in private room. I arrange it."

"Finally!" Dot looked excited. "Pedro, show us to the room!"

Pedro smirked. "Si Señora. Follow me."

As they stood up, two policemen entered through the front door. Pedro drew a deep breath. "Again? What's this?"

Hamish remained calm. "It'll be the Marina business."

Jack went white. "Roger, can you ask them what they want?"

Roger was too late. Jack gulped as the two officers approached. They gestured to him to come with them.

Dot was panicking. "Do something, Roger. Are they arresting him? Can't you go with them? Help him, Hamish!"

Anxiety flashed across Pedro's eyes. "Mr Domingo he no come. He no like police."

Hamish glanced at Roger. "Let's not jump to conclusions. He heard English voices on the day of the incident. It's probably that."

Judy looked up. "That would be Roger and me."

Hamish clicked his fingers. "Of course. That'll be it. Pedro, what's the matter?"

Pedro stopped shaking for a moment. "Not just incident. Marina die. Is it murder? Jack is good man. I no trust Spanish police. I worry for my amigo Jack."

Pete gave a low whistle. "Ok. Roger, Hamish, let's get down to the police station. Dot and Judy, get on with your holiday as best you can."

Hamish's voice was quiet. "Good advice, everyone. This is a simple misunderstanding. It'll be fine. But I'll stay here."

Pete's expression turned to one of alarm. "You need to be with us, Hamish, with your experience."

Hamish shook his head. "If they think I'm telling them what they should be doing, they'll do the opposite. No, Pete, we'll keep it low-key."

CHAPTER 12

Dinner that evening was subdued. Dot's frustration burst out as Pete suggested they all had an early night.

"Pete, I can't do that! Jack's being detained by the police. How you can even think of relaxing, I don't know. I can barely eat."

Roger put a calming hand on her shoulder. "Dot, we understand. He's our friend too. Isn't that right, Judy?"

"He's not being held, Dot. He has volunteered to stay until this is cleared up."

Dot erupted. "You don't get it, not one of you. I'm responsible for this. It's all my fault. If I hadn't believed that prize email, none of this would have happened." She stormed out, brushing past a man with sunglasses who turned with surprise before taking the vacated seat at the dinner table.

"Hello. I'm Mr Domingo."

Hamish was first to react. "You're English. Is that a Surrey accent?"

"Yes. I was brought up there but I'm half Spanish."

Hamish grinned. "Me too but I'm not. This lot think I'm Scottish. I'm Hamish."

"I know."

"Where in Surrey?"

"Surbiton."

"Really? You know, I think we have met before. I can't quite place you, Mr Domingo."

"Shall we say our paths may have crossed professionally, Hamish?" He grinned.

Roger intervened and shook the newcomer's hand. "Glad to meet you, Mr Domingo. You've got some explaining to do, I believe."

"I will tell you what is safe for you to know."

Hamish was unflustered. "That's wise, Mr Domingo. So why are we all here? There was never a competition, was there?"

"No. Let me explain."

Judy stifled a yawn. "Can we get on with it, please?"

"I have a friend. He had to flee from England and he came to the southern coast of Spain. He'd been in jail for crimes which left him with many enemies, and they'd tried to kill him. I met him off a flight to Malaga. He was very distressed. An innocent man had been shot dead in the assassination attempt."

Pete's brow furrowed. "Is your friend familiar with Liverpool, by any chance?"

Mr Domingo shrugged his shoulders. "I just met him by the entrance."

"Ah. One question too many. Please continue."

"In southern Spain there are a few Brits whose identities have changed for, erm, practical reasons."

Hamish nodded. "Running from the past, maybe?"

Mr Domingo ignored the question. "I help such people. They pay me to make arrangements."

Pete folded his arms. "So it was you who orchestrated this charade to bring us all here. Roger and Judy think it's about starting a church down here, Dot thinks she won a holiday and brought me and Jack with her, and Hamish smelt a rat but came anyway."

The man scratched his chin slowly and deliberately. "He wants to see you all. He has to be so careful. He has tried already. The problem is that the police know these kinds of people. They don't want them here. They collaborate with their counterparts in England. Any excuse and they'll hassle them to try to drive them out."

Hamish looked uncomfortable. "So that's why you haven't met us till now. The Marina business."

"That's right. Very unfortunate. It's safe for me now because they are investigating further and have a suspect in their grasp."

Pete stood up. "That's Jack! No way is he involved. You've got to be joking if you're thinking of using him as a scapegoat for your criminal mates. No way!"

Hamish motioned to Pete to sit down. Domingo looked flustered. "No, no problem. It's just a process. It's not even a crime yet. But it gave me the chance to meet you."

The retired detective pursed his lips. "How did you get Jack arrested?"

Domingo gestured towards the waiter. "Pedro. He told them."

Hamish had one more question. "And what part does Pedro play in the underworld you appear to inhabit?"

"Pedro? He's my son."

"But he's Spanish!"

"He's as English as you are, Hamish. He affects not to speak it well around the hotel. Surbiton born and bred. His Spanish is fluent because his mother was from Marbella. He's acting for me in more ways than one, that's all. Now may I continue?"

Pete was having none of it. "How can we be sure of what you say. You arranged this? You and your son organised the detention of an innocent man who is currently stressed out of his mind about what's going on, never mind Dot who is blaming herself for the whole business. Mr Domingo, or whatever your name really is, we're getting out of here as soon as Jack is set free."

"Easy, Pete." Hamish was conciliatory. "Let's hear the man out."

Pete subsided. Domingo took a deep breath. "It's an alibi issue for what probably was an accident. Relax."

Hamish shifted on his chair. "Easy for you to say. Difficult for us to do. Now what does your friend want, Mr Domingo?"

"He wants to do good things. Like he needs to make up for his past. He's talking about God. He's on a mission to bring God to other people like him. He says they need God."

"And do they agree?" Pete's tone betrayed the realism in his mind.

"No. Me neither. But he doesn't give up. And then they are puzzled by him."

"Why might that be, Mr Domingo?"

"Pete, it is how he is. Even I find it odd. He has a peace about him which they don't have. Some of them say it unnerves them. He's making quite an impact. But from you? He wants to know what to do next."

Pete sat back and opened his hands. "That's why Roger and Judy are here, then. But why us?"

"Because my friend says you do good in Liverpool. You feed poor people, you help those with problems. He says churches in Spain are more about rituals, mysteries and dressing up. He told me that you all get your hands dirty. Spain has many problems which are like those in the UK."

"So why the secrecy? Why the cover story?"

"You need to understand the world he and I live in. If those who hate him find any trace of a link to where he is now, his new identity will be unravelled, and he will be in danger yet again."

"Why did he choose to live in the hinterland beyond Seville? Why not downtown Marbella or Malaga?"

"It's proper Spain. Spanish culture, flamenco, tapas, the real thing. No concessions to English beach tourists. It's safer."

"And what does he call himself now?"

"Shaun. Shaun Ivor Davies."

For the first time in a while, Pete smiled. "That's the confirmation I was waiting for."

Domingo looked blank. "What?"

Pete paused for ironic effect. "Better you don't know, Mr D."

Mr D affected disinterest. "I must go. Pedro will tell you where to meet tomorrow. I'll send two taxis at 11 am. Make sure Dot is with you. Oh, and tomorrow you will be moving to rooms in a new hotel, just three doors down from this one. In case this is closed by the police. I'll be paying."

Pete looked inquisitively. "Very kind of you, Mr Domingo. You seem fairly certain about this."

"No problem. On past performance, I'd expect them to isolate the potential crime scene, which means the bedrooms would be out of use. If so, you'll still have your meals in the place you're in now. We can't have you out on the street, you know."

CHAPTER 13

Dot skipped breakfast but caught a glimpse of Roger striding out down the street. She learned the reason for his purposeful gait when Judy, Hamish and Pete emerged from the restaurant.

"He's gone to the police station to find out where they are up to with Jack. You flounced out, knowing his predicament." Judy was in a determined mood. "He wants to know when they will have ruled him out. He's a rather unlikely suspect, don't you think? Does that make you feel any better, Dot?"

Dot's face reddened. "My departure wasn't what it seemed. I had to use a pretext."

Hamish smiled. "You're right to be concerned about Jack, Dot. You're his friend. But sometimes acting on emotion damages your case. Anger is understandable."

"That wasn't it, Hamish. I couldn't explain last night, but the waiter had told me to go to the bar three doors down the road. He said there was someone there to see me. If I'd told you, you would have accompanied me to keep me safe. So I did my flouncing act. Pure theatre."

"Hang on, Dot, Pedro told you? And did you go?"

"I did."

"And who was the man?" Pete's paternalism was unrestrained.

"I can't tell you. Nor what he asked. But he was horrified about Jack. He said he would pull a few strings and get him exonerated. That's more than you were going to do."

"Why you, Dot?"

"I can't tell you that either. I'll compromise Jack's situation if I say anything before they let him go."

It was a full hour before Roger returned. He grimaced as he joined them in the hotel lobby.

"Not good. They know he has no alibi, but there's a link they're looking at. It might not have been an accident. Illegal substances are the issue. Jack was too honest for his own good."

Judy was bewildered. "He's an undertaker, and a Christian man who tries to walk the walk. He seems to have walked once too often, but how come they think he's a drug trader? That's utterly ridiculous."

Roger stared at Hamish. "They're investigating Jack's god-daughter. He told them why he hated what heroin had done to her. She was apparently called Maria, so similar to Marina, the victim's name here."

Hamish stared back. "Rather unimaginative, Roger? Why didn't she call herself something a bit different?"

"Drugs do strange things to people's minds, Hamish. Or maybe it was a double bluff?"

"Maybe. Or a kind of exhaustion with life as she lived it. Anyway, putting two and two together, I think Jack may have confused the interpreter, just when the police were looking for a motive."

Hamish shook his head sadly. "That's not great news. Inter-gang conflicts are one thing, but internal strife is just as common. Jack's an unlikely killer, maybe, but he's entangled with the story. He may have a motive."

Pete couldn't contain himself further. "You don't believe that, Hamish? You know the guy."

Hamish was quick. "Not at all. I'm reading how the police see it. Being an evangelical Christian in Spain is seen as membership of a cult. It's no guarantee of anything. And what better cover than to pose as an undertaker? They don't know he's a real one. And even if they check that, do they know he's not corrupt?"

Roger looked at the ceiling. "We need to pray like never before. Pray that the Lord will strengthen Jack, that he will say the right things and that his name will be cleared."

Judy agreed. "And soon. If the media get on to this story, they'll hound him, even if he's exonerated."

Pedro approached and pointed to his phone screen, then the door. "11 o'clock. Taxis. To Santa Justa area, café near station. You all go. Mr Domingo pay."

Roger stared at him and shook his head in disbelief. Pedro bowed and said no more.

Judy took Roger's arm outside the hotel as they waited. "Why were you shaking your head at Pedro in there?"

"His pidgin English is inconsistent. It's different whenever he speaks. That's all."

Hamish overheard Roger's words. "You weren't there when Domingo claimed Pedro was English born but with a

Spanish mother. As a linguist, are you convinced that Domingo was telling the truth?"

Roger nodded. "Languages are codes. If you speak two fluently, you switch from one to another, like there's a switch in your head. But Pedro's choosing not to flick his switch. He's making it up as he goes along."

Hamish smiled. "The question is why."

CHAPTER 14

Pete's taxi was first to reach the station approach. He opened the back door for Hamish whilst Dot's cab pulled in with Roger and Judy on board. She was on edge. "Is he there? I can't see him. He's not there."

Pete motioned them to a pavement table, but Dot went straight in. Moments later, she emerged with a smiling bearded figure who waved as he approached the group. She grinned. "May I present Shaun Ivor Davies!"

"Sid! It's you!" Judy was effusive. "Come and join us! You've got rather a lot of explaining to do! And not just about the beard!"

"Shaun, my friends. My name is Shaun. Shaun Davies. Let me get some drinks for you. Dot, come and sit by me."

Dot did. Shaun put his arm around her, and she snuggled up to him. When the waiter has taken the order, Roger took the initiative.

"Well, erm, Shaun, thank you. I see you remember Dot."

"I do. Shall I start with that?"

Dot took the initiative, her grin wider than the café door. She chose her words with care. "Shaun and I met up last night.

It was him in the bar by our hotel. We had some catching up to do, and now we have unfinished business. Shaun has asked me to be his girlfriend."

Hamish was unmoved. "You and, erm, Shaun, erm, met in Liverpool, did you not? You spent a few weeks there, if I remember rightly. It was somewhat tumultuous, wasn't it?"

Pete looked around, checking no stranger lurked within earshot. "Sid, one of our Hub members was killed by a bullet meant for you."

"Shaun, Pete. Shaun." Dot reduced her voice to a whisper. "He was Sid. Same initials, new i/d. He's Shaun."

Shaun raised a hand. "Can we move things along? It's not safe for me to stay too long anywhere, even here."

Dot squeezed Shaun's hand. "I feel safe with you."

Pete shook his head. "You might like to think that's the case, Dot, but I'm not so sure."

Hamish murmured in agreement. Judy and Roger sat back in their chairs. Dot's face darkened.

Shaun ran his hand through her hair. "Would you tell them what we discussed last night, Dot?"

She brightened a little. "Shaun keeps saying that he wants to start a version of the Hub near where he is living, close to the coast. He thinks God has been prompting him to do so. He says God sent him to Liverpool to find faith after he came out of prison, that we all helped to change his heart, and now he wants to respond to God's kindness."

Roger leaned forward. "Have you given your life to Jesus, Dot? Have you repented and invited him to be your Lord? I'm so pleased if you have!"

Dot shifted uncomfortably. "Not exactly. Life's been very

challenging and I'm so busy. But I've done more and more for charity though since I met everyone."

Judy was encouraging. "That's good, Dot, but you're missing the point of why. It sounds like Shaun will be able to help you with that, if what you say about him is true."

Dot was keen to return to her agenda. "Yes. But he wants me to be the manager of his new Hub."

Judy frowned. "Shaun, don't you think you need a Christian in that role?"

Shaun shrugged. "It doesn't seem to be a problem in Liverpool."

Roger shot a glance at Pete and moved the conversation on. "We'll come back to that. Tell us more, Shaun."

Dot beat him to it. "He wants to pay for everything. Money is no object. We can start on this today! And there's something else too. It's about Mr Domingo."

Pete rolled his eyes. "Don't tell me, he's paying for your engagement ring."

Dot blushed profusely. Pete apologised with open palms and indicated that she should continue. She did.

"It's Jack. He'll be back at the hotel tonight. They will declare him of no further interest and let him go."

Pete was unconvinced. "He's volunteered to stay until that happens. He can leave when he wishes."

"Mr Domingo is visiting some contacts as we speak. He will see to all matters. Jack will have dinner with us later at the new hotel." Shaun glanced at his phone. "I've a train to catch. I'll meet you this evening. Dot will explain more. Your taxis will be here shortly. Enjoy your day."

Moments later, he was on his way. Two hours later, the rest

of the group had regathered over post-prandial coffee on the terrace of a bar on the Guadalquivir bridge near the bus station.

Pete outlined his agenda. "Let's hear Dot out on this. Then we take a break to consider the proposition individually."

Judy was anxious to interrupt. "Pete, we need to meet together to pray this through once we've heard what Dot has to say. All of us."

Dot looked uncomfortable. Roger realised. "It'd be good if you were with us, Dot. You can come and stay silent."

"That would not be like me." She smirked and looked at Judy. "Can we meet back here before dinner? I like this spot."

Pete approved. "Now then, Dot, take your time and explain what Shaun, aka Sid, has in mind."

Dot leaned forward briefly before settling back. "So it's all good, but can you check I've got all this correct? Shaun had met your old friend Harry when they were inmates, doing time. Harry was in for historic child abuse offences, and Shaun, or Sid as he was known then, was in for serious and serial fraudulent activities."

Judy gulped. She wasn't expecting to hear Harry mentioned by name. There were times when his death was still raw in her mind.

"Harry suffered a lot from fellow convicts, but Shaun told me that Harry had become a Christian. He'd handed himself over to the police to take his punishment. Shaun saw that despite the beatings, Harry had this peace about him, and he wanted some of that for himself. So before Shaun was released, Harry gave him a contact in Liverpool. Shaun believes that this was directly from God."

Roger's eyes lit up. "Yes. And that's how he found the Hub. You had just planned the famous outreach mission when Sid showed up."

Dot's brow furrowed. "Shaun, please. It's vital we call him that. Careless talk could cost him his life."

Hamish agreed. "Practice doesn't make perfect. It makes permanent. Let's remember that. Dot, do go on."

"Ok. It's difficult for me to talk about God in the way you all do, because I don't know him."

Judy stroked her lip. "Just phrase it as you can, Dot."

"Right. So Shaun explained that he'd found what he was looking for and became a Christian. But he was a hunted man. He'd defrauded the wrong folks and there were contracts out on his life. They nearly got him too, but the assassin took out Harry, who by then had served his time and was back in Liverpool. Shaun said that not a day goes by when he doesn't think of him."

Judy covered her face with her hands. Roger read the situation and intervened. "God can forgive everything if people turn back to him and acknowledge their wrong-doing." He looked at Dot. "You don't have to kill someone to do wrong, Dot. Not one of us is able to claim to be free of evil and guilt. But Shaun has accepted Jesus as Lord and has found a new freedom. You can have that too, Dot. It's a peace which is so great, we cannot fully understand its scope."

Dot sniffed. "Never mind your peace just now, let me say my piece. So Shaun had to get out of town quickly. He needed a new life."

Roger wagged a finger. "You can have one of those too, Dot."

Judy had recovered her poise, enough to betray mild frustration with her husband. "Let the girl speak, Roger." He bowed his head in response.

Dot went on. "He headed for Spain, thinking he would be taken for a tourist. What he found was an ex-pat community, not all of whom were there for the sun. Some were fellow ex-cons who had reasons to be out of the UK. He realised immediately that he needed to proceed with caution. It seemed there were self-styled community cleansing guardians, people looking for information they could sell to those with revenge in their hearts, those who were settling old scores on behalf of victims wanting to exact their own version of justice."

Hamish pursed his lips. "They certainly exist. They often fall into the cracks around Interpol co-operation. And they would certainly be interested in the likes of Shaun. Dot, how does Shaun view his move here now?"

"I was coming to that. He's done well so far. He's stayed safe, kept a low profile. He's appointed Mr Domingo to assist him, not that Domingo shares his ultimate vision. Domingo makes his money through some kind of benign and legal protection racket. Shaun thinks he's worth the money."

"Is Domingo trustworthy, Dot?" Pete was curious.

"Shaun says Domingo was sent by God."

"Is his name really Domingo?" Pete was even more curious.

"Don't ask me. It does suit what I am going to tell you next. How do you think Shaun wants to move forward?"

"Leave the country." Hamish was clear. "Get out while he can."

Dot shook her head. "No. He wants to bring God into the lives of these people with a dodgy past. He wants them to find the Lord, as he put it."

Roger looked pensive. "I see. But he can't do that without help?"

"He can't do that at all. Too much profile. Too much media interest. That's why he wants to talk to you."

"Really?"

"He'll pay for it all. He's a rich man, Roger. And when I told him what I did, he said he'd fund a Hub for me to run. And with a good salary."

Roger smiled reservedly. "Ok, Dot, we've got the picture. One last question, though, did he mention Jack?"

Dot's face lit up. "Oh yes. He described him as his best mate. In Jack's words, he was his bezzie. He was very annoyed to hear where he was spending his time on this holiday trip, then told me he'd see to it that he was out and cleared by tonight. Great news."

Hamish did not join the general murmur of approval. "Shaun seems to have become well placed in society in a very short time, Dot. Especially for someone keeping a low profile."

Dot was not for tolerating opposition. "He's a decent man, Hamish. People take to him."

As a former detective, Hamish was an expert at picking his battles. This was not one he would win. He winked surreptitiously at Roger, who smiled.

Judy had a question. "Dot, does his wealth, erm, smooth the way for Shaun to achieve his aims?"

Dot's speech increased in volume and speed. "He's just a

very good man. If you think Jack deserves to be in jail for a crime he didn't commit, then you can be critical. If not, we should all be grateful."

CHAPTER 15

"Jack!" Dot rushed to hug him. "It must have been awful. You've been cleared!"

Jack's smile turned to puzzlement. "How did you know?"

Dot tapped her nose knowingly as the lift opened in the lobby to reveal the rest of the group ready to drop their luggage at the new hotel before heading towards the river.

Jack's return was warmly received, whilst Dot had a message. "Dinner and breakfast are definitely back here, everyone. They're closing off the accommodation floors, but they're allowing existing guests to use the restaurant."

Jack's tone was relaxed. "Thanks, Dot. You all go ahead and get settled in. I'll get my stuff packed and follow you."

Dot glanced at the others before agreeing. "We'll give you ten minutes. See you by the entrance. Then we'll head for the terrace bar."

Half an hour later, Dot was choosing a table. Jack was first to speak. "I passed this place on that fateful first walk. Listen, I've caused you enough worry, let me get the drinks."

"I'll do that." Dot was firm. "Shaun told me that he would pay."

"Who's Shaun?" Jack looked at her quizzically.

"You know him as Sid."

Jack's face turned the colour of astonishment. "Sid! Is he Mr Domingo? I thought it had to be him."

Hamish emitted a low whistle. "No, Jack, steady on. Look, we all have to refer to him as Shaun. He's in danger if his old identity is revealed."

Jack frowned. "Hang on, Hamish, his real name isn't Sid. It's what he was called in the prison. Isn't his name Stephen?"

Hamish put a finger on his lips. "Discretion, my friend. Be careful. He's Shaun. Nothing else."

"Sorry. I forget you aren't really called Hamish. Nicknames stick."

Pete sipped his white rioja. "His victims are still searching for him. They'll have caught up with the previous names he was using. They may not be looking for an evangelical Christian though."

Judy leaned forward to speak, but Roger had already asked her question. "How did you hear you were no longer a suspect, Jack?"

"It happened very quickly. You know I was never held by the police? I stayed voluntarily. I think that helped. They said it was very rare. But nothing happened fast at first. There were questions about my alibi when I was out before breakfast, the time when the poor girl was stabbed. They almost let me go after that. If only they'd found some CCTV with me on, leaving the hotel and coming back later, it would have put an end to things."

Judy needed to know more. "Why were you still of interest to them?"

"Partly because I insisted on staying. They thought it was a bit odd. And it was my own fault for saying too much. I was being honest with them, that's all, wanted my name cleared, but they weren't used to that. They asked me again about Maria. I said she was like a god-daughter to me. And the drugs. They think that Marina was killed in our hotel over an international smuggling feud. They thought the names were too similar and I was the assassin."

"How was that resolved, Jack?"

"I've no idea. The policeman who spoke some English came in and told me they weren't interested in me anymore. So I walked out."

"Simple as that?" Roger shook his head.

"Almost." Dot hesitated. "When I told your old friend Shaun, he said he would pull a few strings. You have him to thank."

"I would like that, Dot. He seems to have got a very slow process speeded up, however he did it. I owe him a drink. Why did he bring us all out here in the first place? It doesn't feel like it was to give us a great holiday?"

Dot explained what she knew. Hamish and Pete disappeared inside, only to emerge rather pensively as she came to the end of the story.

She seized the moment. "So I can't see why we can't press ahead with Shaun's plan. Let's get the groundwork done for a Hub out here. Seville's the perfect place."

Pete coughed. "Don't get ahead of yourself, Dot. He doesn't want it here. He's based near the coast. I'm guessing Marbella way. His concern is to help ex-cons to find faith and salvation, to free them from guilt. Like them or not, there's a community in need down there."

Judy took a deep breath as Pete finished. "There's a lot to talk about, Dot. It's not as clear cut as you think."

Dot's face turned to thunder. "I'm really not sure what you people want. You want to spread your good news and reach new people, but when an opportunity lands on your plate, you don't take it. Fully funded, what's not to like?"

Judy stiffened. "Take it easy. We're grateful to you for all you've done, Dot. Now leave us to do our work."

Pete headed off the developing atmosphere. "Jack, I'm sure you would like to meet Shaun yourself. Let's see if Mr Domingo will fix that up. Let's get Jack's perspective on what Shaun has in mind. Would that be ok with you, Dot?"

She relented. "I suppose so. Jack's his mate. Yes, ok."

Jack acquiesced. "One thing, though, Dot. How did you know I'd been cleared? I'd only just been told myself."

Dot smiled with satisfaction. "You meet with Shaun, and I'll tell you. I'll set your meeting up for tomorrow."

Dinner was a subdued affair. Pedro had taken the rest of the day off, and there was no sign of Mr Domingo or his messages. It was Jack who closed proceedings. "Let's call it a day. We'll meet again in here tomorrow morning."

Dot wasn't at breakfast, but Jack was keen to get on with his task and hot-footed it back to his room down the road, followed by the remaining diners a few minutes later. Pedro had arranged a taxi for ten o'clock. Roger, Judy and Pete were equally keen to ensure that Jack knew their concerns.

Hamish joined them on the hotel steps as Jack returned from his room shaking his head. "No sign of Dot."

Hamish shrugged. "Probably gone out for some fresh air."

Jack sucked in some air. "I hope she's got an alibi."

Hamish's cough implied confidentiality. "I think she may have."

Judy checked her phone. "Let's get on with it. Jack, how are you reading the situation?"

Jack looked startled at being asked the question, before recovering his poise. "So there's something dodgy going on at the hotel, for starters. Then this whole holiday lark was a complex ploy to bring us all together out here. And dear old Dot seems to have access to more information than she should. How am I doing?"

Hamish interrupted. "What about you, Jack? Why have you been picked on to come out here and have the heat turned up on you, if it wasn't warm enough already down here?"

"Me? It's all coincidence. I've paid the price for being honest with them. I'm not linked to a drugs ring, I promise you."

Hamish shook his head. "We know that, Jack. Why was your name cleared? Did they tell you?"

"I presume they had completed their enquiries."

"Ah, fair enough." Hamish hadn't finished. "In my experience, such matters take longer, that's all."

Judy looked perplexed. "Why, Hamish? Jack stayed on a voluntary basis. He was never arrested."

Hamish wagged a finger. "It happens. And it can be a criminal ploy to appear innocent. Just as much need for investigation, just less procedure and paperwork. It'll be the same here as in the UK."

"What are you saying, Hamish?"

"Money may have changed hands." Hamish's tone was firm. "It happens."

"Thank goodness it doesn't happen in the UK. That would be awful." Judy pursed her lips before grimacing.

Hamish raised his eyebrows. "Corruption is everywhere, Judy. It's human nature unfortunately."

Jack smirked. "In Liverpool we say that the UK has the best police force money can buy."

Judy brought the conversation back on track. "Hamish, how safe is Jack if a bribe has been paid?"

Hamish thought for a moment. "In the short term, fine. Weeks, I guess. Maybe longer. After that, it's hard to say."

Roger had been taking it all in. "Let's talk about Shaun's aims. You know the guy well, Pete. Is he genuinely a born-again Christian?"

"I believe so, Roger. He attended a week of sessions around Luke's gospel, and the writer's focus on the vital importance of truth. It's what he'd been looking for."

Jack spoke up for his friend. "It was solid gold. He was a changed man. He committed his life to Christ and accepted the grace of God and his forgiveness. But there was something else happened which I think is relevant. He fell for Dot. Big time. He couldn't tell her then, although I think she suspected something, because of her own safety."

Pete agreed. "She knew something at the time, certainly. Without being cynical, though, I would add that Shaun seemed to be the answer to her problems."

Judy sighed. "That's a typical male attitude. In these situations, a woman's intuition tells her what's right and what isn't. With respect, Pete, I don't think that is relevant."

Jack folded his arms. "Shaun now has a faith. He wants to bring others to share his beliefs, and he wants to do that through relationships. That's what the Hub does. It connects people at their point of need, whether it's foodbank, emotional support or practical help. Of course he is the answer to Dot's issues, but she's not the only one he now wants to help."

Pete sat back. "Good."

Jack stared at him. "What right do we have to sit in judgement over a relationship between Shaun and Dot? It's none of our business."

Judy intervened and lowered her voice. "Jack, you're a leader as we are, and I think you know better than that. A pastor guides the sheep along the right paths. It's certainly confidential, but it's absolutely our business. It's simply up to the sheep to decide if they want to follow what we say."

Jack flinched at Judy's correction, but he hadn't finished. "He's genuine. He needs us to help start a Hub community for the expats down here. As Dot indicated, the finance is there. The money comes with the mouth."

Roger paused for thought before breaking the ensuing silence. "What is its source, Jack? That's the question."

"I'll ask him." Jack's reply sounded curt. "Just because he did time doesn't mean his cash is corrupt."

Judy looked at the time on her phone. "The taxi will be here before we know it. We'll reconvene this evening."

CHAPTER 16

"Two hours in a taxi, Sid! That must have cost you a bomb!"

"Great to see you, Jack. It's Shaun, if you don't mind. Sorry you had to wait for me to collect you."

"No worries, mate. There was shade where the driver dropped me. How have you been?"

"Jack, I'm doing well. It's a great place to live. Orange trees by the house and olive groves everywhere around."

"I never saw you as an olive farmer, Shaun. This is beautiful, if rather remote."

"No-one can find me here, Jack. But I'm only renting the house. The neighbouring farmer manages the harvesting and the oil sales. I've seen him in the distance, but never met him. Remote is good."

"Ah, that must be why the taxi didn't drop me at the door."

"Exactly. Now I imagine that I owe you a few explanations."

"You do, my friend. Starting with this plan of yours."

"In a moment. Two things to begin with. Firstly, I'm sorry

you wound up in the police station for so long. I was very distressed to hear that."

"It wasn't what I normally do on holiday, for sure."

"I've more to say on that later. Secondly…."

Shaun was interrupted by a female voice from the kitchen. "Coffee, Jack? Same as usual?"

Jack looked bewildered. "Is that who I think it is?" Moments later, a figure he knew well appeared in the door frame.

She grinned broadly. "Afternoon, Jack! With a biscuit?"

Jack gulped. "Dot! What are you doing here?"

Shaun didn't allow her to answer. "We'll come to that. Dot, come and join us on the terrace when the coffee is made."

Five minutes later, the three of them were seated around a rustic table. Jack sat in the shade whilst Shaun and Dot shared a bench in the noonday sun.

Shaun began slowly before gathering pace. "I have had to take some serious steps to protect myself since I left you. After Poor Harry's murder. He was used by God to point me to finding faith, and it cost him his life. I've beaten myself up so many times for letting that happen, and not a day goes by when I don't think of him."

Dot smiled weakly. "I told the others that, Shaun, while Jack was with the police."

Jack waved his hand in a vague gesture of support. "I know Shaun well enough to know that's true, Dot."

Shaun returned Dot's smile and continued. "I talk to God every day and am reading the Bible. I'm in Acts at the moment, seeing how the church was started. I've referenced Revelation to it, and God has put it on my heart to bring more people like Harry and me to himself. How do I do that? The Hub, plus you guys, are all I know. So I set about getting you all over here."

Dot coughed. "After we'd accepted through this competition prize ruse, Shaun got in touch to see what my feelings were. They matched his. I just couldn't tell you anything, Jack, or I'd have blown the cover."

Shaun sniffed. "Dot's not going back with you. I'll make things right with Pete, but she's staying."

"Pete will cope, don't worry. So you two need a bar code."

"Why so, Jack?" Shaun looked at his friend.

"You're an item."

"I shouldn't have asked. Will that news mean the others won't meet with me, though? We aren't married."

Jack left a dramatic pause before replying. "They're not going to be over-excited by that, but they'll need to see the big picture. There's one issue that is pre-occupying them, Shaun. It's where your money is coming from."

"Ah. That's complicated. I should have foreseen that one. I can't pretend I didn't go to jail for fraud. Financial fraud, blackmail, I did it all. I'm not a good bet in their eyes, Jack, I see that."

"I'm not judging you, mate. You want to do something beautiful for God. Dot's very keen on your plans, I know."

Dot nodded energetically. "Just think of the good it can do."

Shaun looked at her. "I hope you'll become a believer one day."

Dot reverted the conversation to the previous topic. "You don't know where Shaun's wealth is from."

Jack wasn't having it. "That's as may be. And I now know how you knew about my release. Shaun, have you told Dot about your past, you know, before you went to jail?"

Dot intervened. "He's told me the lot. Honey traps for high profile figures, usually involving sex, to make great headlines. He told me they weren't best pleased when they were exposed, so he has a lot of enemies. Some of them are powerful."

Shaun shrugged. "It was a form of extreme journalism. It sold papers back in the day. The stakes were high. Later, ok, I got into blackmail to keep the stories hush hush."

Jack smirked. "Never mind the money issues, I'm not sure your past makes you an ideal contender to be the next Archbishop of Canterbury."

Dot held up her hand. "Easy, Jack. Shaun's mother passed away a few days after Harry's murder. He's her only child. She never lost touch, even when he was in jail. She was a church-goer in London, she prayed for him every day."

"It's ok, Dot. Jack's my friend. I needed to see Mum, to thank her, to tell her I was planning to put everything right about my past, but I couldn't risk going to London. It would have been playing directly into the hands of my enemies. They knew where she lived. I phoned her, said I would go when I could. She didn't tell me she had a terminal diagnosis. Never put her own problems first. That was typical of Mum."

Jack put his hand on Shaun's shoulder. "Sorry, mate. She sounds like a wonderful mother."

Shaun sniffed. "I let her down. Single mum. Ran her own business and brought me up. Sent me to boarding school. Business thrived. Then I started to get into trouble. I felt rejected by her, you know, emotionally. She had time to think once she retired, found a church to attend, and then regretted her negligence of me as a child. By then it was too late to save me from what I had become."

Jack patted him again. "Church-goer? Was she a Christian?"

"Of course, Jack."

"Going to church and doing good doesn't mean she was, my friend."

"Not sure, Jack. I believe she was very much a woman of faith."

"I know yours is strong, mate. You have a personal relationship with Jesus now."

"I do. The cross means he's forgiven me for all I've done in the past."

Jack stroked his chin poignantly. "Your heart is in the right place, my friend. I'll give you that. How can I help you to move forward?"

"You report back to Roger and Judy what I've told you. Mr Domingo will come in the morning. Then tomorrow, we can all meet in his friend's house near the Plaza de España. If they want to. He will send taxis for you as usual. Everyone will think you are sightseeing."

"I'll do that for you, Shaun. I will be there, even if they are not."

"Thank you, Jack. I do miss our beers together, putting the world to rights. Maybe you can come out here one day when it's safer and spend some time with me and Dot."

Jack was taken aback. "That's it, is it? You're here for good, Dot."

"Yes and no." Dot's face was alight with excitement. "I'm

staying a few weeks to begin with. But I've still got stuff in my hotel room. Can I come back with you now, Jack? I'll go back with Shaun after tomorrow morning. Then I'll be back in a month or two to close down my affairs in Liverpool, if all has gone well."

Shaun nodded. "I'll drop you off where I picked you up earlier. The taxi will arrive a few minutes later. You can wait in the shade there, Jack, and Dot can enjoy a few rays. Remember not to speak of me on the way back."

Jack frowned. "The driver?"

Shaun looked at him. "Can't be too careful."

The car journey passed, the silence broken by outbreaks of polite conversation. Shaun was not mentioned by name. Jack was aware that the nature of his own friendship with Dot was evolving, and he might soon be surplus to her requirements.

It was after 9 pm that evening when they gathered in Jack's room. Dot stayed in hers. Jack began the conversation.

"Sorry it's a bit cramped, but this is for your ears only. I'll keep it short. I checked him out. Firstly, he's living life in a remote farmhouse on an olive grove. Secondly, I was right when I told you he's genuine. He spoke of making up for his past. He has a real heart to do God's will and to spread the gospel which saved him. He's reading about the early church in Acts at the moment. Thirdly, he's a wealthy man. He's behind everything we've experienced so far. It's him who has been paying our bills. He's keeping a very low profile with the aid of Mr Domingo. Finally, there might be some issues about his money. Oh, and he wants to meet up tomorrow to take his plan forward."

Jack sat back. Roger rubbed his hands together

enthusiastically. "What does he know about starting a Christian organisation, Jack?"

"Only what he's gleaned from us. Hardened fraudsters don't usually have a remit to plant churches, especially while they're behind bars."

"Would you say his view is born more of enthusiasm rather than experience, then?" Judy was anxious to soothe Jack's anxiety.

"Yes, Judy, that's fair."

Her comment had worked. "So he needs our experience to match his energy and drive?"

Roger followed suit. "Good work, Jack, that's helpful. Would you say he has looked into the costs of his plan?"

Jack pursed his lips. "Not too much. He's got plenty of money, though. He wants to do the right thing."

Pete looked thoughtful. "Give to Caesar what is Caesar's, give to God what is God's, eh? He will have read that. Luke's gospel."

Judy looked up. "That was about taxes. How is his dodgy money God's?"

Jack sighed. "Caesar isn't much of an option these days, anyway."

Roger winced. "He's got to keep out of sight, but there are always ways. What about Domingo? He seems to fix most things."

"Any kind of big spending attracts attention. And how far does Shaun trust him with more than petty cash?" Pete was subdued.

"Domingo won't know too much." Hamish was certain. "I know his type of operation. Always in the grey areas of life, the shadows. The less they know, the better. I'd say he's not an option for this side of things."

Roger agreed. "If only his money was legal."

Jack waved a hand in the air. "Dot's convinced it was. He was employed by the media at one time. Good salaries there, you know."

Hamish looked at him. "Jack, if I remember rightly, didn't that line of business involve setting up honey traps to bring down high profile figures? Wouldn't that be a problem ethically, even if it was taxed by the Revenue?"

Pete got in first. "I suspect we'd have a problem there. It'd leave us ourselves keeping a low profile, never mind Shaun. Tainted funding and God's work don't mix."

Judy gasped. "Enough said. We can't touch this project with a barge pole."

Roger puffed out both cheeks and exhaled slowly. "I'd go further. We have a duty to stop it. God's name is to be honoured, not besmirched by scandal. Unless there's anything else Jack can tell us, of course."

"There's one thing that won't help if the media get a hold on this. I forgot to mention Dot. She's not coming back with us. She's staying on with Shaun. They're in a relationship. Unmarried. It's about judging them. The media will murder us in a Catholic country like Spain if they find that little nugget, however hypocritical it is."

Pete smiled. "So she's staying, is she? She knew more than she was letting on, I guess."

Jack nodded. "With good reason, Pete. The more she said, the greater the risk to Shaun. But I imagine it's curtains for his big project."

Roger shook his head. "Not exactly. Dot's vulnerable to the attraction of wealth, as her past proves. What if his money was attracting her into rushing into decisions which she'd later regret?"

Jack looked at him. "You're not saying he's cynically creating a trap for her, I hope?"

"Not at all. I'm saying that he is a Christian brother who has asked for our help, and she is vulnerable. We have to help."

Judy perked up. "Agreed. We need time to think. Positivity is what we need. Pete, Jack, this is a huge pastoral issue. Will you let us meet with Shaun? You need a long chat with Dot. She needs to see what she's getting involved with here, and you are her friends."

Pete gave a thumbs up. "I'm good with that."

Jack sounded a note of alarm. "Shaun's planning taking her back with him after the meeting tomorrow. From what we know, it could all end in tears. We'll have to talk with her in the morning, see if she'll change her mind."

There was no need to wait until the morning, as at that moment, Dot strode in. "Evening all." Her words and tone took Jack briefly back to childhood evenings with Dixon of Dock Green, but one look at Hamish brought him sharply to the present.

Dot pre-empted his response by carrying on. "I hope you've agreed to Shaun's request. I've been speaking to him in the last hour and for a grown man, he is so excited at what can be achieved."

Roger moved to head her off at the pass. "We've agreed to meet him tomorrow, Dot, but please don't build up your hopes too much. There are a few issues to resolve." He looked around the room. "We will all be praying about them together. You are welcome to stay for that. Otherwise, let's leave it at that."

Dot headed back to the door. "I don't get you lot. What is there to pray about? Shaun says God is telling him to do this. I'm not sure what else can be achieved."

Jack was conciliatory. "I know it's difficult for you, Dot, but an open mind would serve you better. I hope that one day you will understand what prayer really is. All we want is for God's will to be done, but we need to discern it first. That's all. Now why don't you stay and at least listen? Please?"

Dot opened the door. "Can't, Jack. He's calling me back in five. There's so much to talk about. But I'll let him know that tomorrow is on." A moment later, she was gone.

Pete smiled. "At least we seem to have a direct line to him at last. Now let's pray."

CHAPTER 17

Pedro was on duty when Hamish led the way through the lobby to breakfast. Pete was right behind. "Hamish, I'm going to ask him to speak proper English. There's no need for pretence any more now we know who's who and who's done what."

Hamish stopped in the corridor. "I don't recommend that, Pete. We don't know the half of it yet. Let him do things as he sees fit. Don't compromise him."

Breakfast finished, Pedro confirmed the taxis for the Plaza de España. "You have a half of hour to look round then Mr Domingo, he find you. He take you to the house."

Dot blinked. "I'm going direct. I'm taking my luggage to the house. I'm checking out. I'll come back to reception here shortly, Pedro."

The waiter looked at her. "No need, I know this. I come to your hotel to carry suitcases. Mr Domingo tell me yesterday."

Roger put his serviette down. "It's beautiful, Dot. Some amazing ceramic work to see. You can't miss it, surely! You'll just love it."

Dot was not for turning. "See you at the house."

Jack grinned. "What's the address, Dot? In case we don't see Domingo?"

Dot refused flatly. "No way. Security, as you well know, Jack. No chance."

An hour later, Domingo led them into the doorway of a small house a few hundred metres and several streets away from the Plaza. He ushered them into the kitchen where, moments later, Shaun appeared. Jack sensed he was in a state of anxiety.

"Shaun, my friend, pull up a chair. Relax."

Shaun did as bid and looked at Roger who opened in prayer. "Lord, thank you for bringing us together to seek your will in such a beautiful city. May it be your voice we hear most clearly throughout our discussions, and may the outcome be to your honour and glory."

"Amen!" The murmurs of assent came from all bar one, but after a glance round the room, Dot said the word too. Jack acknowledged her with a smile.

Soon, though, she was speechless. As Roger explained the pitfalls discussed on the previous evening, Shaun backtracked on every aspect of his plan. Roger praised his commitment to responding to God's grace, and then asked him a question.

"Shaun, in your enthusiasm, might you have overlooked how church planting works? I think you may have."

Shaun bit his lip. "Tell me what's going on in France. You were in Paris, weren't you?"

Judy took over. "Not from the start, Shaun. We took over once the church had been planted."

"Did you run a Hub there? For the community?"

"Paris is different, Shaun."

"I adored Paris when I was younger. You must have loved working there. The food, the wine, the culture, the history, the style, the elegance. The Latin Quarter, Notre Dame before the fire. Where did you live?"

"Suburbs. A bit of a concrete jungle if I'm honest."

"You must have travelled in a lot to see the sights. I bet you got some real insider knowledge about where to eat and what to see. Did you use your free time to travel more widely? I loved Normandy too. Especially the cider and that wonderful smelly cheese, Pont something or other."

"L'Evèque? It means the Bishop. Bishop Bridge."

Shaun chuckled. "Sounds like a purple-shirted card game. Did you go there?"

"No. Actually we only went into the centre of Paris for meetings. We lived in the community we served."

Dot clucked. "You must have had some time away."

Judy laughed. "We had family and friends in England. We visited them." Her face straightened. "We weren't in France as tourists, Dot."

Shaun shrugged. "I guess you couldn't. You were there to do a job. Was the area you lived in quite bourgeois?" He looked pleased with his choice of term.

"Not exactly. It was mostly concrete. Flats. High rise. We had one. It was the side of Paris you don't see in the holiday brochures."

Dot screwed up her face. "Didn't you have a choice? You could have moved."

Judy stared at her and lowered her voice. "We chose alright, Dot. We chose to live there. It's not like the UK, you know. Churches need street cred to be taken seriously. They need to empathise. Not just sympathise. No, Dot, God is looking for foot soldiers for his campaign plan, not half-hearted dreamers or tourism-minded retirees."

"That's exactly who Shaun is looking for too." Dot was set to argue her corner. "Can't you see that?"

Roger smiled weakly. "We see that, Dot. But Judy is hoping you will have a deeper understanding of the implications of his ideas, so you can see what your own role might be."

Dot relented a little. "I can be rather hasty, I suppose."

Roger's smile broadened. "We all can. It seems to me that Shaun has a major role for you, Dot. You wouldn't want to find yourself unable to deliver what he is asking for, whatever and wherever that was, would you?"

There was still a trace of reluctance in her reply. "No, not really. Can I remind you that I am used to working in a Christian project and I try to be as supportive as I can? Jack knows that since he was asked to oversee my work. I admit I don't always manage it, but even as a non-believer, it's not an alien concept to me."

Pete spoke up for her. "Since she joined the Hub, Dot's been an absolute trooper, if I can use another military term."

Dot's grin was short-lived as Roger held up a hand. "Not really, Pete. There's an important difference. A trooper has support because the cavalry is fighting alongside. But Shaun's project has no cavalry. Dot's role requires a Christian. As Judy says, a foot soldier."

Shaun broke his silence. "I pray that Dot will come to know her maker through her role with me. But I take your point, Roger."

"I'm not saying she can't be involved, Shaun. Of course she can. And we will pray that she will be saved through the gospel she will hear as she works."

Dot's face witnessed her partial relief. "The same pay, Shaun. That's a red line for me."

Shaun nodded. "No worries, love."

Judy refocussed the meeting. "The money is a major problem, Shaun. We cannot be launching a mission on what people perceive as illicitly gained funding. We know your motives are fine, but any evangelical church plant will inevitably be seen as a weird sect by the media, and probably the authorities too. If they suspect anything improper on the financial side, they will enjoy tearing everything we do apart. It can't happen."

Shaun accepted her point. "I read the parable of the rich young man who couldn't give up his wealth, so I wanted to do what he wouldn't. Lately I've come across Ananias and Sapphira in Acts. Scary."

Jack had been listening intently and now he was ready to contribute. "Would a developing church be a better option for Shaun than starting from scratch? Dot is used to that from her time with the Hub."

Roger was first off the mark. "Yes, but it still leaves the financial matters to resolve."

Judy turned to her husband. "Let's set them aside for the moment."

Shaun agreed. "Tell me about the realities of church planting. And what you do now."

Dot looked at Judy suspiciously as the latter began. "Our strapline is 'supplication, supplication, supplication'. The planting, the nurturing and the blossoming need constant prayer, Shaun."

Dot couldn't hold back. "I don't get that. If God asks you to do his work, why do you have to ask him for the resources? If he's as powerful as you say he is, he'd just provide what you need."

Roger raised a hand. "Let Judy continue, Dot. You really do need a deeper understanding of what prayer is. You and I can have a chat later."

Dot subsided somewhat. Judy flashed a smile in her direction before going on. "Shaun, you've scratched the surface of a huge challenge with your idea. France and Spain are actually part of the largest mission field in the world. Europe desperately needs the gospel."

Dot's tone was more subdued but equally determined. "Those countries are Catholic. Just look at how they honour God here in Seville, fabulous processions, real fervour. Just because these people don't belong to your denomination isn't a reason to fight them."

Judy's patience was exemplary. "I agree. But ritual and tradition can be empty of meaning without genuine and personal conviction."

Shaun grinned. "The judge gave me one of the those when they put me away. But here, you mean the personal relationship with Jesus Christ. Right?"

"Right."

Shaun softened his voice. "Dot has a point, Judy. So many people are put off exploring faith because of the wars which have been fought over it, no more so anywhere than in this part of Spain. I'm not sure about the Catholic country thing, though. From the limited amount I've seen, it's a bit like Christmas."

Jack raised an eyebrow. "Explain, Shaun."

"These days for most people, Christmas has lost its meaning. Ask them why they are celebrating, and they can't tell you, except because it's Christmas. Same here in Seville with the fiestas. Faith isn't just for Christmas, it's for every day. Look at the churches in Spanish towns and cities and they are empty most of the time."

"Same in France." Roger spoke with authority. "Beautiful churches with historic architecture everywhere you go, but life, heart and vibrancy? Like the congregation, they're hard to find."

Judy gestured towards Dot. "We welcome the fact that some of the Catholic churches work with ours. From lending buildings to us to generally supporting what we do. We welcome that."

Shaun wanted to know more. "That's how it should be. So in France, what exactly do you do?"

"It depends on the community we serve. Each church is different. Each generation is different. Each month is different. We seek to do God's work, to be his hands, in the lives of those he sends us."

"And is it thriving, Judy? It sounds good."

"At the moment, Shaun, a new evangelical church is planted in France every ten days. God is very much at work there."

"When you say a church, you don't mean a building, I take it."

"No. I mean a community. Where they meet largely doesn't matter."

"And what does a church plant require beyond that?"

"Leaders. And supporters."

"I can see funding implications here, Judy."

"Indeed, and that's not all. Leaders need training. It's a specialised field. Pastors may need Bible-based training as well as language skills, never mind the social media skills required these days. It's a long process. We need to treble the number of students coming forward if the mission is to flourish. The number of places at Bible colleges needs to expand too. More facilities, more buildings, more maintenance, more trainers."

"There's much to pray about, Judy." Shaun glanced at Dot who looked down.

"There is, Shaun. And so much for which we are thankful. We receive regular prayer and financial support from so many warm-hearted folk in the UK. They keep us going."

Roger concurred. "They are the body of Christ reaching out to those in need, in every sense."

Pete smiled. "There's synergy with the Hub here. My mother would be amazed by your work, Judy and Roger, and those like you. The way you operate is the best way to counter the marginalisation of Christianity by society and its culture."

Roger rubbed his hands together. "Never more so than in France. The laws separating the state from religion have impacted us heavily. But God is good! Christianity is now cool among young people, because becoming one is an act of rebellion against authority. And that's what Jesus did!"

"He did." Judy went on. "Working people are generally confused as to what religion, as they see it, really is. They are most affected by the culture, and it's harder for them to make a radical change which could alienate themselves from their friends and workmates. They see the world's problems, for sure, and tend to agree with the need for tolerance and inclusion but seem generally rather lost as to the solution. A strong evangelical online presence is important for them, especially for young people. It is often their first step towards finding truth. YouTube, videos, social media. We had one student in her twenties who came to us via this route when we worked in Paris, asking to be baptised."

"What about the older generation?" Pete was curious.

"Typically, they develop what we call N.A.S. Noah's Ark Syndrome. They mentally board the ship to be saved whilst the flood is raging."

"Major life events affect all ages, of course." Roger's face changed. "Funerals, weddings, childbirth, divorce. People often re-evaluate life at those times. The number of evangelical Christians has increased one hundred per cent over the last thirty years and is now around one per cent of the population."

Shaun's tone rose a little. "There must be a tipping point coming. The snowball is rolling. That's very encouraging."

Judy gave him a thumbs up. "There is still so much to do. We need more people backing us with prayer and finance, people encouraging potential leaders to apply. We need more creativity behind the scenes, fresh impetus too, but God's love is coming like an avalanche to France."

"And Europe." Roger opened his arms expansively to make his point.

Judy hadn't finished. "There are so many issues in French society which I guess are Europe-wide. The polarisation of opinions and the personal attacks on whoever ventures a view which is not popular are going on here as well as elsewhere. The rise of right-wing extremism and the legitimising of policies which used to be beyond the pail, widespread support for appalling attitudes towards refugees, and issues with the police are leaving people wary of promoting debate and discussion. They end up confused as to what to believe is true."

Dot grimaced. "What about women's rights?"

"That's another problem, Dot. There has been some progress, yes, but the attitude of those in authority to domestic violence, rape crimes and sexual aggression is often found to be verbal only, and there is a deep and embedded resistance to investigation and prosecution. For us Christians, we struggle to make ourselves heard in the abortion debate. Abortion is now a right enshrined in law, and we are not permitted to generate discussion around the matter, or even put other options to women whose circumstances have led to them seeking a termination. That cannot be healthy."

Dot sat back. "Those issues are sometimes linked, aren't they? Abortion is an easy way of dealing with a problem without solving the root cause."

Judy shook her head. "Abortion is never an easy choice, Dot. The psychological damage frequently exacerbates that done by the unpunished wrongs that led to the pregnancy in the first place."

Roger nodded. "Society is riddled with confusion more than ever before. The wider statutes of the state have been made more important than God's laws."

"I understand the problems, Roger, but what's the answer?" Dot was genuine.

"Reliable and relevant Bible teaching, Dot, together with prayer for those whom society has placed a smokescreen over truth. Reaching out to those on the margins, the victims of injustice, the disadvantaged and the unloved. Meeting them where they are and supporting them through their difficulties."

Judy looked thoughtful. "We should pray for the perpetrators too. At every level."

Shaun looked approvingly. "This is a much bigger deal than I realised. Judy, I love what you've just said. Praying for enemies and those who have harmed you is so hard, but it's such a powerful way of dealing with the issue."

Judy smiled. "We don't get the option as Christians, Shaun. We pray to the Father for forgiveness of every wrong we have done, and we have to do the same to those who have hurt us. It's the body of Christ in the world."

Shaun leaned forward. "The body of Christ is more active than I realised, Judy."

Judy smiled again. "Let me show you this from another angle. The missionaries who actually go out to do the work need to feel strongly connected to the mainstream. The grapes need their vine. They often face situations which are way beyond their comfort zone. I can tell you it could feel very lonely. We're only human, after all. Knowing there are hundreds of supporters cheering us on year in and year out with their prayers and their financial support is huge. We are so grateful to them, Shaun. They make a bigger difference than they will ever know."

Dot was nonplussed. "Now I'm confused. Bodies, grapes, vines. But how can I be involved if I'm not a Christian? It leaves me on the outside."

Shaun placed his hand on hers. "We'll talk about that, Dot. I was in exactly the same position when I met Harry in jail. He had a peace about him which I could only envy. I was an outsider, wanting to spend time with a man who was locked up for abusing his own daughter."

Tears welled up into Judy's eyes. Roger made to put his arm around her, but she pushed him away. "No, Roger, I can deal with this. The man you are speaking of, Shaun, found forgiveness when he turned to Jesus and committed to turning his life around. Later, he handed himself in to take his punishment. His guilt was dealt with on Calvary. I struggled with it for some years, especially after he tried to come back into my life. He went to glory after being murdered for someone else's crime, not his."

Dot's insensitivity was too much. "Isn't that good news for you Christians, in a way?"

Judy sobbed. "You appear to have forgotten that I am that daughter, Dot."

Roger's arm went instinctively back to his wife, who accepted it. He knew that she had never before been able to say those words so publicly. Her healing was almost complete.

Dot gulped. "I'm sorry, Judy. I've got so much on my own mind. I don't know what to say."

Shaun closed his eyes for a moment in silent prayer. As he finished, his phone vibrated in his pocket. A quick glance and he stood up. "Must go. There's been a problem. I'll take the time to think through your comments. Dot, you're coming with me. The rest of you, enjoy Seville. Domingo will cover any expenses until you leave."

CHAPTER 18

It was Domingo who saw them out, Dot having left with Shaun as soon as he had finished speaking.

"There's no way we can accept any more from the man. I mean Shaun, not Domingo. Domingo is just the hired hand." Judy motioned to Hamish, Pete and Jack to join her on a bench in the elegant frontage of the Plaza building. Roger remained on his feet. Domingo gave them a final wave in the distance and turned his attention to his phone.

Roger agreed with his wife. "We shouldn't have been so foolish, coming out here. If Shaun had wanted to do something honourable with his ill-gotten gains, he could have done it without having all this charade going on."

Hamish sniffed. "I'm not so sure. He's vulnerable, remember."

Roger looked down at the group. "True. He's also a new Christian. He's obviously evangelical in his intentions. I think he's genuinely reached out to us for help."

Judy looked cross. "I'm sure he is and I'm sure he has. It's not the man that is the problem, he's been forgiven by the Lord. It's what he's doing. He is well-intentioned, but we're playing with fire taking his hospitality. This is a scandal we have brewing. We're living off the proceeds of crime."

Jack had been listening carefully. "Judy's right, but I think we're missing the point. Dot's gone off with him. Don't we have a responsibility to bring her back? We can't just leave her exposed to what we're running away from. She needs help. And so does Shaun. Let's give him till tomorrow. We're flying home then anyway."

Judy looked towards the road where a police car had pulled up. Two officers emerged and walked off towards Domingo. "There we go. He's in it, for sure. Up to his eyeballs."

To her surprise, the three of them appeared to be speaking amiably. Domingo pointed towards their own group, and they walked towards them at a brisk pace. Domingo approached first and shook Jack's hand. Moments later, Jack was in the back of the car, heading to the police station. Domingo was nowhere in sight.

Pete was first to find some words. "What's that all about? Talk about a traitor's kiss! I'm in shock. Did you see the handshake?"

Judy nodded furiously. "Oh yes. I knew we shouldn't have got involved. Poor Jack."

Hamish waited his moment. "Let's not jump to any conclusions here, not on anyone or anything. Let's get back to the hotel and talk it all over."

Judy was horrified. "So one of our brothers has been falsely arrested, and we're just going to discuss it, are we?"

Hamish was about to retort a reply when Roger stepped in to head off a conflict of opinions. "Judy's right about action. Hamish is the man with the experience. We don't know why they've taken Jack back in yet. So we need to do both."

Pete weighed in on Roger's side. "We have to be prepared to think the unthinkable. We don't know everything about Jack, even though he's a friend and a brother. At the same time, we need to support him. Innocent until proven guilty, remember."

Judy was incensed. "How we can even think that of Jack, I have no idea. We've got to get him out of there and get all of us home. The longer we're here living off someone's illicit earnings, the more trouble we're making for ourselves."

It was Hamish who came up with a plan. "Roger, you go to the police station. With your Spanish, make sure the police get the proper story of what Jack meant when he told them everything. The rest of us, let's go back to that café on the bridge and go over all we know. I'll pay for the taxi."

Judy remained frosty. "Yes, and I'll buy the drinks. The last thing we want is Shaun paying with his tainted money via Domingo."

Pete nodded. "You don't think Domingo will pay more money to get Jack out again, do you?"

Hamish was clear. "No, I don't. But let's get to the café. I'm not comfortable discussing it out here. We don't know who may be watching us."

CHAPTER 19

The café terrace offered a table discreetly away from other customers, and Hamish indicated his satisfaction. Judy ordered a large bottle of mineral water and after the waiter had poured the drinks and departed, he opened the discussion.

Discretion took him to Judy first. "What's your take on this whole business? The holiday that wasn't, the outreach which couldn't be done, Shaun's funding of it all? We know your views on Jack."

"Yes, he cannot be guilty. He's too nice a man. He's got a heart of gold. Roger and I have talked a lot, and we cannot see him carrying out a murder. No way. The level of his care and concern for Maria, his god-daughter, is awesome."

Hamish intervened. "Not really his god-daughter, Judy, but I know he said he prayed for her so much."

"That's right. I said awesome, and that makes it even more so. Jack described her to me as a scruffy druggie with blue hair, and I know his heart was for helping, not judging her."

Pete raised a finger. "Judy, he wasn't able to help her much, as I remember. It was Dot who became involved."

"Took over, more like."

"Ok, but Judy, we need to ask a question here. Isn't Jack's reaction a bit over the top? He gets a request from someone who attended our outreach week to help his daughter, and soon he's calling her a god-daughter. That's not normal, is it?"

Hamish affirmed Pete's doubt. "In my experience, we would see that as in need of explanation if we were seeking a motive. No more than that, depending on what we discovered. We'd do a character assessment."

Pete tapped the table. "If it came to that, Jack would be on firm ground. He walks the walk, he's a Christian man, and consistent in a desire to help his community. He couldn't do the job he does without compassion."

Hamish agreed again. "Totally." He paused before shrugging his shoulders. "But as Christians we still make mistakes or get into a mess over stuff. My gut feeling is that Jack is innocent in this case, but I can't tell you to rule him out. It would appear that the Spanish police haven't, and they must have good reason."

Judy controlled her anger. "We should look at Dot. She's not a Christian. None of us has known her as long as we've known Jack."

Pete smiled. "There's plenty happened since we appointed her to the Hub. She's shown her true colours in my view. She's hard-working, loves being busy, likes leading a team, can be overbearingly enthusiastic, and is short of money since her divorce."

Judy didn't smile. "And can be quite angry about Christianity, if what I hear is right. Scratch the surface and you'll see who is at the centre of her life. She is."

Pete had to agree. "We pray that she'll stop rebelling

against what surrounds her, to be fair, but we have stuck with her. She needs healing, and I hope we have not passed by on the other side."

Judy relented slightly. "Ok, but how did Jack feel when she steamrollered a take-over of Maria's case?"

Pete pursed his lips. "Not happy. He felt that he was meant to be doing this, not Dot. I did wonder if he thought he knew who Maria's father was, the one who sent that anonymous text."

Hamish leaned forward. "Pete, would that by any chance be our good friend Shaun?"

"I did ask myself that. Jack would have known him as Sid, of course. They were good friends when Sid was with us."

Judy clapped her hands together. "Of course. That proves it. Jack's motivation was to help his friend. End of!"

Hamish was cautious. "Not completely, Judy. However, in his favour, I do gather that he wondered if Dot was telling him the truth all the time. Remember she could be said to have a romantic interest in Sid."

Judy smirked. "Shaun. Romantic perhaps, financial for sure. He's minted."

"Jack told me it's genuine alright, Judy. I think Sid, sorry, Shaun, had fallen for Dot, and it was probably mutual."

"Don't you think it odd, Hamish, that Dot has disappeared off with him now? There must have been some contact between them prior to her coming out here?"

"Jack tells me she denied that, Judy. In fact she told him the opposite. What you say, though, is right. Most people would need time before committing to a semi-permanent relationship. It has to be a question we need to answer."

"She's not here to tell us now, Hamish. If she's as hard to reach as Sid, or Shaun as he is now, we risk never seeing her again."

Pete had been listening intently. "We'll refer to him as Shaun. It'll save a lot of difficulty."

Hamish agreed. Pete's face became set as he spoke. "Let me change tack for a moment. Three of us came out here thinking Dot had won some kind of holiday and we should tag along. Hamish, you were suspicious but were drawn to join us. Judy, you and Roger were invited to discuss what seemed to be some kind of church planting project. Are we saying that Shaun was behind all that? If so, why did he have to go to the lengths he did to assemble us all in Seville?"

Judy had calmed her mood. "It does look like him, using Mr Domingo to keep matters as untraceable as possible. Domingo is a fixer who is quite slippery, I would suggest. He comes across as a reasonable guy, but I wonder what is in his past?"

Hamish looked up. "I asked an old friend for a favour on that, a colleague who is still on the force. I told him my vague recollections of coming across a guy just like Domingo during an interpol operation. I was right. My contact got hold of his real name and checked him out. It was complex, but Domingo is just the cover name he uses for working with Shaun. He chose the name Domingo because Shaun likes his Sundays. Our Mr D is now a reformed criminal according to his social media posts who does good for society."

"Why was he in jail, Hamish? Was it something similar to Shaun?"

"No. He was a drugs wholesaler, and not the sort which supply pharmacies."

"Has he really reformed, Hamish?" Judy's tone was insistent.

"Hard to say. The police view is probably not, but that tends to be the way they see proven criminals anyway. I have seen it happen, though. Occasionally, they learn their lesson. Certainly, Domingo was acting on orders from Shaun, and using money as instructed. He doesn't seem to have been filtering funds off for himself, not from what we've seen."

Pete acknowledged Hamish with a thumbs-up, but had another question. "Didn't he hand Jack over to the police earlier today? How does that all square up?"

Hamish thought for a moment. "Do you recall the time when he told us we were moving hotels? I thought he seemed certain of what was going to happen at a time before the hotel staff even may have known. That was not the action of a cautious man looking after his guests. It's nothing significant in the case, but the fact that he knew gives him away. He may have a connection with a dodgy detective, perhaps in exchange for leads from the underworld. Who knows? He could be leading a double life on the fringes of the ex-con ex-pats, maybe in exchange for leniency from the police over something from his own past. It happens."

Pete was less sure. "Or could Jack have been sacrificed by Domingo to get himself off the hook?"

Hamish raised his eyebrows. "Possibly, although given what Domingo now does for a living, it's more likely that he could have been paid more to get someone else off the hook than the cash Shaun gave him the other day to have Jack released."

Judy had one final question. "We're talking about Marina's

murder, aren't we? Isn't that while Jack was out for a walk? Did he not tell us that he went past this bar?"

Pete nodded. "He did. You know all that. Why do you ask?"

Judy shook her head. "Nothing. I'm just going to pay the bill."

As they left the terrace a couple of minutes later and headed back, Roger's wife was looking slightly smug as she directed her gaze at the broad river flowing to the bridge beneath their feet. The Guadilquivir twinkled back.

CHAPTER 20

Back in their hotel room, she spoke in a low voice to her husband. He made a phone call in Spanish and smiled his satisfaction to his wife.

Their final day dawned. The breakfast room was full. The original hotel had re-opened and bristled with life.

"Did you sleep well?" Pete welcomed the others to a newly cleaned table by the window.

"You'll need one more place, Pete." A voice he knew boomed across the room.

"Dot! What are you doing here? Where's Shaun?"

"Back at home. Domingo rang him to say Jack had been taken in again. I told Shaun that I had to get back here. He agreed immediately and got me a taxi. I got the last room back in this hotel, but it was the middle of the night when I arrived. I had to be here. Let me order some coffee for us all."

Judy looked at the new arrival rather coldly. "Hello Dot. Are you thinking of joining us on the flight home today?"

Dot shook her head. "Not if Jack isn't on board, no. Shaun says he'll pay for me to stay here until Jack is released. That man has been a bit of a rock since Shaun left us back in the UK. Shaun knows how much Jack has looked out for me."

Judy lowered her voice. "Did you tell Shaun since you met up again here?"

Dot smiled. "Incessantly. And I've been telling him every day since he left Liverpool."

Hamish scratched his ear. "Ah. And how did you do that, Dot?"

Realisation of her error dawned on Dot. "Erm, I talked to myself as if he was there. It was how I got through missing him."

Judy couldn't hold back. "Dot, we weren't born yesterday. I think you've got some explaining to do."

Dot turned beetroot-red and stood up to leave. She got as far as the door of the room, which opened as she approached it. The twin figures of Roger and Jack blocked her exit, and she returned to the table.

Before anyone could react, Roger seized control. Urgency was in the air. "The train's in an hour. We're on afternoon flights to the UK, so let's eat while we talk." He looked at Dot. "Pleased to see you here. I assume you are not needing a train ticket to Malaga Airport."

Dot looked at the floor. "Maybe not. Listen, has Jack been released or has he been completely cleared?"

Roger couldn't repress a yawn. "Apologies, we've been up all night. It's both, Dot. They've got their suspect under arrest."

Judy could hold back no longer. "Did Shaun's dirty money pay for this, Dot? Did he up the ante and buy his freedom? Is that why Domingo was with them in the car?"

Dot didn't know. "Which car? What do you mean, dirty money?"

Roger stepped in. "Domingo didn't attempt that. I have been with Jack and Domingo all night at the interviews. The suspect finally admitted his guilt a couple of hours ago."

Judy was stunned. "Jack did?" Dot squeezed her hand.

Roger's tone grew stronger. "No, I've told you, he's in the clear. They found an alibi. Your idea in the bar he walked past, you know, when you paid the bill."

"The CCTV?"

"I told the police soon after. They checked it out and found Jack walking past at the time of the death. It took a while. But they got the result shortly before they made their move to seize Domingo."

Jack took up the narrative. "That's right. Judy, you were an absolute star. They didn't want anything more from me than giving my name and address." He glanced out of the window. "They've just arrested Pedro. They're putting him in the back of the car now. He's handcuffed."

Judy peered out. "We knew he was dodgy. His brand of English was a performance."

Jack was quick off the mark. "They can't arrest you for that, Judy. But he may be Domingo's son, which is also not an offence normally carrying a custodial sentence."

Dot seized her moment. She didn't like the direction in which the conversation was heading. "What's going on? What's happening? Judy, can you tell me?

Judy stared at her. "You orchestrated this whole story about the holiday, didn't you, Dot? You were in touch with Shaun the whole time. The whole business was a fake."

Dot's feisty side could not be contained. "We did. Because it was the only way we could get you all out here at the same time. And I foolishly thought that you and your husband would be delighted to be funded for a new Christian project like the Hub. But you needed each other to make it work, Shaun said."

Pete was gentler. "Dot, what did you tell Maria? What advice did you give her? And why did you take it all away from Jack?"

"I regret that. Shaun was furious with me."

Pete was not to be deflected. "What did you tell her?"

"I used my experience to help. I told her she needed a new identity and a new look, and a new home. A new country."

"Just like Shaun did?" Jack perked up.

"Yes. I smartened her up, changed her hair colour to blonde, and dressed her in new clothes. I used my theatre background to create a new character."

Hamish winced. "Did you address the real issue, the drugs, the dealer, the abuse?"

Dot shook her head. "No. I thought that would sort itself out for her. I thought it would all go away."

Roger grimaced. "The thing is, Dot, this side of events was also to do with a plant. And that plant was Maria."

Jack was incredulous. "She was a fake? Roger, how could Shaun's daughter be a fake?"

"She wasn't his daughter, Jack. She carried the evidence of drug abuse. She was made to take on what was an evil mission. She is genuine, tragically."

A look of resignation crept across Dot's features. "I meant well, sorry."

Roger nodded. "You'll be more than sorry, Dot. Maria's new look fooled everyone."

"Not me. I never saw her new look." Jack was irritated. "How could that have fooled me?"

"She called herself Marina. She was the girl on reception."

"I never clapped eyes on her. She was never there when I was. You say that was Maria? I can't believe that."

Roger held up a hand. "It's true, Jack."

Jack thought for a moment. "I suppose it fits the bill. She'd know I was here if she was the receptionist, so knowing when to keep a low profile wouldn't be that difficult. Maybe you're right. Caution probably meant it was better for her to avoid me even after Dot's costumer makeover handiwork."

He looked at Dot who shifted uncomfortably and avoided eye contact. "That was down to me. I warned her to leave her old life behind, including you, Jack. She obviously listened. It was best for everyone."

As Jack shook his head in disbelief, Hamish leaned across and looked at Roger. "So am I right, the hotel was linked to the drugs ring? What about Marina? Maria, I mean."

"The final piece fell into place this morning, not just with arrest. Shaun was a part of it, but unwittingly. He's not in trouble. No, Domingo had his finger in plenty of potentially dodgy pies for sure, but he loved this project with Shaun. Shaun was an easy target."

"Target? Shaun?" Dot held her breath.

"Domingo worked with the international drugs ring, and not just to serve the coffee. The hotel was a convenient front for what they did. The police have been aware for some time of unusual activities there."

"So why didn't they act sooner? Like as soon as Maria was knifed?" Dot was still bewildered.

Hamish was concise. "In any gang set up, they need to get the people behind what happens, not just those who carry out the operations."

Roger agreed. "And that is what happened here. I'll come to Maria in a moment. Yesterday's arrest was a trap that even Shaun would have been proud of. Jack wasn't the target, he was the bait. The CCTV had eliminated him, but Domingo was unaware of that. He was tricked into what he thought was assisting the local police with Jack's re-arrest, but they were actually after Domingo. The slippery villain fell for it hook, line and sinker. He realised that the game was up this morning."

"So why were you really there overnight?" Judy was looking relieved.

"The police didn't know who was watching. They didn't want any further suspects leaving town."

"And Maria?"

Hamish was first. "In the drugs case I mentioned, records showed that he was estranged from his daughter. They fell out after Domingo was locked up. She was referred to as Maria back then. Let's stick to that, as it's probably her real name."

Dot swallowed hard. "But Maria told me in confidence that it wasn't her proper name. I believed her."

Jack squirmed. He was still struggling with what Dot had done and couldn't look her in the eye. His voice betrayed reluctance. "She was a bit vague with me about that. I didn't give it a second thought."

Hamish looked puzzled. "Nothing to worry about. The

police will have all that worked out. Don't give it another thought."

Roger had nearly finished. "Thanks Hamish, that's helpful. They did fall out, the imprisoned father and his daughter. And it stayed that way. She got hooked on drugs, though and found herself trapped in the world she had entered. That part of the story was correct."

Hamish's face displayed a professional satisfaction. "Roger, well done. One thing, though, what did these illegal narcotics racketeers want with Jack and the Hub?"

"Jack will remember the drug dealer in Liverpool who took her own life. He told Dot all about it. Her death broke a link in the supply chain. As soon as he heard, Domingo sent Maria's partner over to take charge of his interests and to find a replacement."

Hamish broke into a smile. "That makes sense, Roger. Is there anything further?"

"Yes. Domingo obviously knew what Shaun wanted to do with his money. He did some research on the Hub and mentioned it casually. Shaun took Domingo into his confidence and told him about Jack. So Domingo found Jack's number, messaged him anonymously, and the poor girl was forced to go over on a mission."

Jack smiled. "An outreach of a rather different nature to ours."

Roger's speech slowed. "It was. Domingo is a cynical, calculating criminal and a virulent atheist. His aim was to discredit the Hub and to put a stop to Shaun's dream of an evangelical church plant in Southern Spain."

Jack let out a low whistle. "So I was right, there was a real father behind that message. I have to admit that I immediately thought it might have been Shaun, operating with extreme caution."

"There's more, Jack. Pedro had never accepted her as his sister, and enmity had brewed for years. It all blew up when the Liverpool plan went askew."

Pete's brow furrowed. "How so, Roger?"

"It seems Maria had become increasingly desperate. She was the victim of an abusive so-called partner who was regularly raping her. Domingo sent them both to Liverpool to replace the dead girl. Her partner took charge of damage limitation over the funeral. He met Jack, of course. He told Maria to research him, and she found the Hub. Domingo knew about Jack already, as Shaun had mentioned his name in conversation. That was Shaun's big mistake."

Pete's brow remained furrowed. "Go on."

Roger did. "The Hub would have been an ideal front for Domingo's narcotics trade, and an undertaker approaching retirement on the minimum wage could have made the perfect new dealer. But on the website was the story of a man whose life was changed by meeting Jesus. Maria found it, read it, and wanted that for herself. She figured out that you, Jack, would be able to help."

Jack looked in disbelief. "So Domingo thought I would be vulnerable to illegal financial gain, safe from the authorities, and Maria considered me able to help her spiritually?"

Hamish intervened. "Liverpudlians don't have a great reputation in some parts of Europe. Work-shy tricksters and benefit scammers. I'm afraid Domingo may have tarred you with that brush. Right, Roger?"

"Yes, Hamish, the police have discovered that there were pump-priming funds available to help get Jack onto the operation once Maria's partner had prepared the ground. As you've heard, Jack, your age and occupation were the perfect cover."

Jack picked up Dot's look of alarm and set aside his disappointment over her treatment of him. "Dot saved me from that. I will be forever grateful."

Dot acknowledged Jack's generosity of spirit but Judy shook her head. "I'm not so sure. Remember Jack could have led Maria to salvation and eternal life."

The words struck home. Dot's morale hit rock bottom. She spoke two words under her breath before leaving the room. There was an underlying bitterness in her tone. "Thanks, Judy."

Jack followed her out whilst Hamish had unfinished business. "Roger, I'm guessing that when Dot in her wisdom ensured Maria left the country, she came back here in a worse mental state than before."

"She was, Hamish. Even her identity change gives that away. Maria becomes Marina? It was as if she was past caring. But in Liverpool, Dot kept her away from everyone but herself. Maria wanted to know about the gospel, in effect, but Dot had no intention of delivering on that score."

Hamish had more to say. "And I'm also inferring that in her state of mind, she was on the verge of revealing the entire set-up to the police. That's why they've seized Pedro. When Domingo realised what was about to happen, he told our waiter friend to silence her permanently."

Roger shook his head. "Not at all."

It was Hamish's turn to look puzzled. "What? Are you saying Domingo carried out the murder himself, Roger? That's not his style, surely."

"Absolutely not, Hamish. Pedro was in Seville to keep a low profile for a while in what looked like a proper job. Whilst Maria had abandoned her father, Pedro hadn't, and was rewarded, if that's the word, with a role in the drugs set-up once the prison sentence was over. But Maria? They certainly didn't see eye to eye, but Pedro didn't kill her."

Judy looked at the group. "Dot's going to need a lot of help. I've been stupid, haven't I, speaking so plainly. But you're going to tell us that Maria took her own life. Please let me be wrong."

Roger looked at his wife. "It's not your fault, my love. Witnesses told the police that there was an argument up on that fourth floor on the fateful morning. It was in English. Pedro and Maria both spoke native English, of course. They'd argued before breakfast when she was on duty in reception, she'd threatened to do what Hamish guessed. She went up there to escape him, but he'd followed her and trapped her in the maintenance store there. He made his point forcefully and left her, but it was all too close to how she'd been treated by her abuser. She killed herself with one of the saw blades."

CHAPTER 21

Two weeks later, Judy started the Zoom meeting as Roger came in from the Breton community room which they used for worship. Hamish signed in from Surbiton, whilst Jack was a guest at Pete's house as his host did likewise.

Social niceties over, Jack's host began with a prayer before Judy asked the obvious question. "Is Dot joining us?"

"She's elsewhere." Jack was diplomatic.

Judy didn't push the matter. "So did the Hub survive the week without you?"

Pete grinned. "Just about. A group of members did a great job, although they don't want to do it again for a while! How's Brittany?"

"Beautiful, as always. It's good to be back. We've been contacted by a local man who wants to bring his family along. He's seen the website."

"Sounds good!" Pete was upbeat. "Any upcoming stuff we can pray for?"

Judy nodded. "There is. We've got some migrants around, and the town isn't keen on helping them. They have come to us for practical support but resources are very limited. We rely on our donors to stay with us on the journey, more than ever."

Pete knew the problem. "It's happening all over. People who have more than they need want to protect their riches, not share them. We get some of that round here, though it's worse in other areas of the UK. People have been so misled. Have you any good news to bring us?"

Roger moved to the centre of the screen. "Actually, we do. We're on the south coast here, but there's a church plant on the horizon with one of our partner organisations. Have you heard of a place called Perros-Guirec? It's a few kilometres from there."

"Heard of it! I love it! I was there a month ago, if that! That's amazing!" Pete was elated.

Roger opened the palms of his hands. "They've asked us to help set the project on its feet."

"Count me in, Roger! Can I be involved? What can I do? What do you need?"

"You're part time, my friend, remember, and you are needed where you are, Pete, in Liverpool. Remember your mother's wishes."

Pete wasn't having it. "My mother would be thrilled if she knew what her dream had brought us to. The Hub has just run itself for a week without me and Jack, and it's still in one piece. I'm in, Roger. Never mind part time, I'm in! And the Hub community will support us. That's what Liverpool folks are like. Generous to the last."

Judy returned to the topic of Dot. "We were hoping she'd be with you. We've got some news for her."

Jack explained. "She's been very downcast since we came back. She told me she was looking to move elsewhere, but no-one seemed interested. She's broken-hearted after her hopes of a life with Shaun in the Southern Spanish sunshine were dashed. He says that he's no longer safe now she's told him the truth about Domingo, and he needs to move on."

Judy's voice rose. "That's why we need to speak to Dot. Shaun sent us a message earlier."

Jack took the initiative. "I hope it's a kind one. She knows she's made a mess. Judy, she is planning on resigning."

"I hope that's not down to me. I came across very harshly, I fear. But she didn't treat us with honesty throughout the whole issue. What's your take, Pete?"

"It was a serious breach of trust, if we look at it in the cold light of an English morning. She can't stay long term, I agree, but we need to give her time to find another job. There's a notice period, of course. We can't throw her under a proverbial bus."

Judy moved the conversation forward. "We've had some very good conversations with Shaun over the last few days as I mentioned. He's come up with something which might help here. He was hoping Dot would be with us so we were all on the same hymn sheet afterwards."

Jack was hopeful. "Leave that with me. She's a survivor. Let's hear it all first. Did Shaun listen to what you told him about church planting?"

Roger coughed. "We missed one matter, but basically, yes. He sees the true nature of a church plant project."

Pete interrupted. "Can we know what you mean by that, Roger?"

"Of course. A planting project needs to be sustainable spiritually and financially. It's not sorted by throwing a load of cash at a building, it's so much more. It needs plenty of support."

Judy took over. "It needs prayer and an openness to going where God wants us to be. It needs to be the body of Christ behind it. Forget the glamour, there is none. Building the kingdom is hard labour."

Roger affirmed his wife's comments. "That means we can't define the problems we want to deal with. Society has never been more divided, God's laws have never been so challenged, and we need to be led by the people he sends us."

Pete wondered where this was all going. "What is Shaun's view? Is he still as passionate about sharing his faith?"

Roger was alive with joy. "He is, and he's so relieved. He's been studying Acts, and came across the story of Ananias and Sapphira, who were struck down dead for lying about money. They were keeping some for their own purposes. He thought that applied to him, that he had to give everything to God or he would face God's wrath."

Judy glanced at Jack. "We helped him understand that story, and that changed everything."

Jack couldn't wait. "So cut to the chase, what's he proposing, Judy?"

"He's going to find a new name to go by, and a safe place where he can buy a home. He's going to propose to Dot. He's thinking somewhere with holiday let potential."

Jack looked relieved. "He's been watching too much daytime tv, that man."

Judy hadn't finished. "He wants Dot to run the business with him. It has to be near a new church plant project too, Jack."

"With its own community Hub? Dot can do that too!" Jack clapped his hands together.

"No, not straight away, it's too close to what's gone wrong in her life. He hopes she'll find the Lord, and then maybe that'll be the time."

Pete looked at Roger. "What was the issue we'd missed?"

Hamish spoke up before Roger could answer. "I'm guessing it's to do with the money. They will simply support the new church out of the income they earn from the business, so it's all clean."

Roger raised a hand. "No. Shaun will fund the purchase of their Hub."

Hamish looked astonished. "With dodgy funds. You can't do this. Anyway, who would want them?"

Roger grinned broadly. "We have spoken to our colleagues involved with the new plant and explained the situation. They would welcome Dot and Shaun into their project. It won't be immediate, though. In a few months, probably. These things take time."

Hamish stuck to his guns. "Then they are foolish. It's still tainted money, wherever they go and however it is laundered. Judy was right about the Spanish project, but that surely applies to this one. We cannot allow this."

Roger's grin became ever broader. "On the contrary, we can. You know what, we never asked Shaun about his money. We all assumed it was ill-gotten, but we were wrong. He has repaid all those he exploited, every penny. The money he has comes from the sale of his mother's house in London. He would be honouring her with his idea. Now where have we heard of doing that before, everyone?"

There was a brief murmur of assent. Judy looked at Jack. "Can you get Dot to join us via her phone? I assume she's at your Hub."

A minute later, a rather embarrassed Dot signed in, and Judy put her in the picture. Jack wanted Dot's reaction.

She thought for a moment. "I'm stunned. It seems like I've won the lottery."

Jack couldn't hold back. "You have, Dot. You've got some time to get ready too. This is an answer to prayer. We'll have you believing in God sooner than you think."

Dot looked pensive. "I've been thinking about the Zaccheus story you told me weeks ago, Jack. I'm empathising with him, guilty and dirty inside. Is that me now? It might be. You also gave me the illustration about the zoo. That's easier. I am the gorilla in your zoo story, Jack. I've landed in the lion's den."

"Let me help you, Dot. How about you feel like Zaccheus when Jesus went to dinner at his house?"

"What do you mean, Jack? Why should I be blissfully happy?"

"You'll find out when Shaun gets in touch. He's got news."

Roger was still purring about Dot's quantum leap towards faith and curious how she had made it. "That's amazing. Will you tell us the zoo story, Jack?"

Dot grinned. "I'll sign out now. Once is enough. Pete, listen out for the trainer's name."

Jack raised his hand. "That wasn't his real name. I've changed it. Now he's called Shaun."

ACKNOWLEDGEMENTS

Special thanks go to Hilary Skinner for her tireless work as editor, and to Dr Phil Johnson for going above and beyond in helping shape the final text. There are no better analytical proof-readers than Jane and Laurence Bozier, and no finer cover artists than the wonderful Lucy Christian. Boundless encouragement has come from Lorna and George Cockayne, Margi and Roger Lewis, Gen and Simon Blackwell, Ann and Mike Shevlin, Chris and Mike Smith, Caroline and Rachel Adamson, Mike Reid, and as ever, the indomitable Judy Sloman.

Gratitude also is due to the inspirational Rachel and Jonathan Vaughan who provided invaluable insights into the reality of life today for those in the European mission field, and Dr Paul Cooke's kind endorsement of the novel is very humbling.

The book is dedicated to them, and all those who have committed themselves to bringing the great news of the gospel to a wonderful continent which so needs to hear it afresh.

Printed in Great Britain
by Amazon

40261527R00088